VICTORIA GRACE

Courageous Patriot

VICTORIA GRACE

Courageous Patriot

ELEANOR CLARK

HONOR✠NET
THE HONOR NETWORK

Dedication

T O MY GRANDCHILDREN AND GREAT grandchildren. May you recognize, love, and appreciate your rich Christian heritage and the privilege of living in America, which was founded on the trust and hope we have in Jesus. May you continue the legacy.

Prologue: School Days, School Days 1
Chapter 1: One-Room Schoolhouse 13
Chapter 2: Doc Finney 23
Chapter 3: Whispers of War..35
Chapter 4: Freedom and Courage 47
Chapter 5: The British Are Coming! 59
Chapter 6: Big Girl, Big Decisions............................71
Chapter 7: Off to War! 81
Chapter 8: True Patriots 95
Chapter 9: Renewed Commitment 105
Chapter 10: Tending the Wounded 115
Chapter 11: Courageous Women 129
Chapter 12: A Wounded Soldier.................................139
Chapter 13: A New Friend..149
Chapter 14: The Homecoming....................................159
Epilogue: Courage 173
Fun Facts and More...181

To my Lord and Savior, Jesus Christ, who has blessed me with the greatest family, life, and country. May every word bring honor and glory to Your name.

To my publisher, Jake Jones, who recognized the potential of my stories and my heart's desire to bless and encourage young readers to value their American and Christian heritage.

To my writer, Janice Thompson, who understood my love of history and breathed life into my stories with the skill of her pen.

To Annabelle Meyers who helped develop the character lessons.

Be strong and of a good courage;
be not afraid, neither be thou
dismayed: for the LORD *thy God is*
with thee whithersoever thou goest.

—JOSHUA 1:9

"I'm going to tell you children a true story that began over two hundred years ago, so listen carefully."

SCHOOL DAYS, SCHOOL DAYS

*S*ARA ELIZABETH LEANED HER ELBOWS against the school desk and looked around the colorful first-grade classroom. All of the children seemed to be having a wonderful time listening to Mrs. Frazier at the front of the room—all but Sara Elizabeth. Though it was her second month of school, she was still homesick.

She didn't like going to such a big school, and she didn't like being away from her mother all day long. Though she had admitted it to no one, she was even a little scared. The older kids seemed so big, and she was concerned that she might get lost on the school grounds.

With a sigh, she leaned back against her seat. "I *want* to like school," she whispered to no one but herself, "but it's so hard being away from Mama." In her heart, she just wanted to be home. Why couldn't this school be like the little church school where she had attended kindergarten last year? Why did this school have to be so… so…*big*? And why did her class have to last all day long?

"Sara Elizabeth," the teacher's voice rang out across the room. "Would you like to solve the math problem I've just written on the board?"

"Ma'am?" She looked up at the chalkboard, realizing that her imagination had carried her far, far away.

"We were working on addition. What is fifty plus twenty-five?" Mrs. Frazier asked, pointing to the numbers written in chalk on the large green board.

"The answer is seventy-five," Sara Elizabeth replied, smiling. At least she always seemed to know how to solve the problems. That made coming to the "big school" a little easier. If only she could get over the loneliness part, everything would be great.

Just then the lunch bell rang, and Mrs. Frazier dismissed the class to go to the lunchroom. Sara Elizabeth trailed along behind the others, listening as they chattered merrily. On any other day she might have joined in, but today she just missed Mama too much.

As they rounded the corner near the cafeteria, a familiar voice rang out. "Sara Elizabeth! May I join you for lunch?"

Sara Elizabeth looked up with great surprise into her grandmother's smiling face.

"Grand Doll!" she said, clapping her hands in glee. "You've come to see me!"

Her grandmother nodded, and as she did, her white curls bobbed up and down. Her big brown eyes glistened merrily as she said, "I told you I would come when you least expected it, remember?"

"Yes ma'am," Sara Elizabeth said as she grabbed her grandmother's soft, caring hand and gave it a gentle squeeze. "And you picked today of all days! How wonderful." She whispered the next words: "I've had a hard morning."

Her grandmother wrinkled her nose a bit. "I've had a hard morning too," she whispered back, "and I needed to see my little Sara Elizabeth to make me smile." She gave her a little wink. "I'll tell you all about it later, but right now let's have lunch with your friends, shall we?"

"Yes, please!" Sara Elizabeth leaned in to give Grand Doll a big hug, suddenly feeling much better. "Will you sit with me at the lunch table?"

"Of course."

As they made their way into the noisy lunchroom, Sara Elizabeth proudly introduced her grandmother to her new friends. They all smiled as her grandmother told them the story of why all of her grandchildren called her "Grand Doll."

"When Sara Elizabeth's cousin, Jennifer Jean, was little, her father used to call her 'doll,'" Sara Elizabeth's grandmother explained. "One day she came to see me, and when she tried to say the word "Grandmother," it came out "Grand Doll." Ever since then, all of my grand-children have called me Grand Doll."

"Really?" one of the girls asked.

"It's true," Sara Elizabeth said. "She's been my Grand Doll forever, and my cousin Jennifer Jean named my grandfather Poppie."

Everyone started chattering, and Ashley Sandifer, one of Sara Elizabeth's classmates, leaned over to whisper in her ear. "Your grandmother is so much fun."

"I know," she whispered back, "and she tells lots of fun stories too."

Grand Doll followed behind Sara Elizabeth as they sat at the table. Sara Elizabeth opened her lunch pail and pulled out a sandwich. "Want to share?" she asked her grandmother.

"Certainly! I just love school lunches!"

"How long has it been since you were in school, Mrs. Clark?" a freckle-faced boy named Chandler asked.

Grand Doll laughed aloud. "Too many years to count! But things have changed a lot since then. Now, if you want to hear a really interesting story, I could tell you about my mother, Bobo, who attended school in a one-room schoolhouse."

"Wow," Chandler said. "Really?"

"Yes, really." She flashed a broad smile. "Children of all ages gathered in one large room and learned together."

"They did?" asked a little blonde-haired girl named Carson Cotton, her blue eyes growing wide.

"Yes, that's right," Grand Doll answered as she gave Carson's hand a squeeze. Soon all the children began to talk merrily about what she had said.

Sara Elizabeth leaned over to whisper something in Grand Doll's ear. "May I tell you a secret, Grand Doll?"

"Of course."

"I don't like coming to this school," Sara Elizabeth confessed. "It's so big, and the older kids scare me a little too. I just want to stay home with Mama. I miss her so much."

"I understand how you feel," Grand Doll spoke quietly, "but school can be a lot of fun if you give it a try."

"I guess." Sara Elizabeth shrugged.

"I know starting something new is hard, but the hard things make us strong." Even as she spoke the words, Grand Doll looked a little sad.

"What's wrong, Grand Doll?" Sara Elizabeth asked.

"Oh, honey..." Her grandmother gave her hand a gentle squeeze, and her voice softened even more. "I told you that it's been a hard morning for me too. I just came from the nursing home, where Poppie has gone to live. It was very difficult to leave him there, but I know it's for the best. He's been so sick." Grand Doll's eyes brimmed over with tears, and Sara Elizabeth reached to give her grandmother a hug.

"I'm sorry, Grand Doll," she spoke softly. "I know you'll miss Poppie just like I miss Mama."

Her grandmother brushed away the tears and smiled. "Yes, sweetie. You miss your mom and I miss Poppie." Tears covered her lashes again. "Missing someone you love is never easy, but the Bible promises us that God will help us through the hard times. That means He will help *you* each day at school, and He will help *me* each day when I'm at home."

Sara Elizabeth sighed as she thought about that. Somehow it made her feel better already.

"Would you mind if I shared a verse from the Bible with you?" her grandmother asked.

"Right here? In school?"

"Right here in school." Her grandmother smiled. Her grandmother reached into her large bag and pulled out a big black Bible that looked to be very old. "The verse I'd like to share with you is from the first chapter of Joshua, verse nine, and it goes like this, *Be strong and of a good courage; be not afraid, neither be thou dismayed: for the* LORD *thy God is with thee whithersoever thou goest.*"

"God is with me…here? At school? In Mexia, Texas?"

"He is. He's with you everywhere you go. When you lay your head on the pillow at night, He is there. When you wake up in the morning and get dressed for school,

He's there. And when you're sitting in your classroom, He's right there with you too. He will give you the courage you need if you ask."

"That's so cool, Grand Doll." Sara Elizabeth grinned. "God comes with me to school."

"Yes, He does, and you can face your fears with courage. Remember, the Bible also says in Philippians 4:13, *I can do all things through Christ which strengtheneth me.*"

"*I can do all things through Christ which strengtheneth me.*" Sara Elizabeth smiled as she quoted the verse.

Just then Chandler interrupted their conversation with his cheerful voice. "Mrs. Clark, were you just teasing us about the one-room schoolhouse?"

"No, I wasn't." Grand Doll shook her head. "One-room schoolhouses are an important part of American history. Why, from the time this country was first founded, boys and girls came a long way on foot to sit and learn in a one-room schoolhouse. Little ones, big ones…they were all there together. And my great grandfather taught in one of the first schools in Texas."

"Did the children learn addition?" Carson asked, her nose wrinkling. "I don't like addition very much."

"Oh yes," Sara Elizabeth's grandmother explained. "They learned a great many things. But children in early America certainly had a lot of other things on their minds besides school."

"Like what?" Ashley asked.

"Well, many of them had only lived here a short while, and they missed their friends and family members in Europe. And in those days, children had to work hard to help their parents too."

"Europe?" Chandler asked. "Where's that?"

"Halfway across the world from America," Grand Doll explained. "Many early Americans came from the country of England and still followed English laws. But most Americans wanted to be independent—to have their own country. That's when the war for independence began."

"War?" Chandler's eyes grew large.

"That's right," Grand Doll said. "Haven't you learned about the American Revolutionary War yet?"

The boys and girls shook their heads as Grand Doll looked at them, amazed. "Why, that's where America won its independence from England! One of Sara Elizabeth's relatives of long ago—a little girl by the name of Victoria Grace—actually lived during the time of the war."

"Really, Grand Doll?" Sara Elizabeth asked.

"Really, and I would love to tell you all about her," Grand Doll said with a happy smile. "In fact, Mrs. Frazier has given me permission to come to your classroom to tell the story this afternoon."

"Really?" Sara Elizabeth's heart swelled with pride. She could hardly wait for the others to hear her grandmother's stories.

The children returned to the classroom, and Grand Doll took the flag in her hand to begin. "I'm going to tell you children a true story that began over two hundred years ago, so listen carefully."

Sara Elizabeth nodded, and so did the others. Grand Doll clapped her hands in excitement and began to share a truly amazing tale. The first few lines caught everyone by surprise. "This is a war story," she began, "and during one of the famous battles, these words were spoken: 'Don't shoot till you see the whites of their eyes!'"

"I love school. I wouldn't miss it for anything."

ONE-ROOM
SCHOOLHOUSE

SURRY COUNTY, NORTH CAROLINA
FEBRUARY 1775

ICTORIA GRACE SKIPPED INTO THE ONE-room schoolhouse with her lunch pail in her hand and sticks of firewood in her arms. After the playful eleven-year-old set the pail down, she made her way through the crowd of familiar boys and girls to the center of the room. There, alongside her brother Todd and the other children, she laid her wood in the pile and warmed her hands in front of the pot-bellied stove.

"It's so c…cold this morning," she said to her best friend, Adeline. "I wanted to stay under the covers."

"Brr! M…me too," Adeline agreed with chattering teeth, "and I'm tired of walking all that way from home. It feels like miles, especially when it's snowing outside."

"Still," Victoria Grace added, "I love school. I wouldn't miss it for anything."

"I love it too," Adeline agreed, "and my mother says we are fortunate to have a school."

"That's true," Victoria Grace said. "Many towns don't even have one. My mother and father didn't go to a school at all."

"Nor mine," Adeline added. "They learned to read and write at home. Mother says once she learned to read, she read every book she could get her hands on and learned a good many things."

Both girls shivered and then turned as the school-marm rang the bell, signaling the start of class. "Take your seats, children," Miss Cuthbert called out.

Victoria Grace removed her wool coat and mittens and hung them on a peg at the back of the room. She then took her seat at the tiny wooden desk that was second from the front. Adeline gave her a friendly wink as she sat across from her. From the desk directly behind her, Johnny Gainsborough sat with a sheepish grin on his face.

Right away he tugged on Victoria Grace's braid and muttered, "Teacher's pet, teacher's pet." He spoke just loud enough for her to hear but no one else.

Victoria Grace turned, and for a minute thought about sticking out her tongue at Johnny, the pesky fourteen-year-old, who always seemed to make fun of her.

"No, I won't do it," she whispered to herself. "I won't let him get my dander up."

She turned with a determined smile to face the front of the room as the lovely teacher took her place before the class and, in a beautiful voice, called out the date—"February 2, 1775."

Secretly, Victoria Grace wanted to look just like Miss Cuthbert when she grew up. If only she had the same golden blonde hair and blue eyes instead of red hair and green eyes.

"Everyone please rise for the morning prayer," Miss Cuthbert instructed.

As all of the children stood to pray, Johnny whispered a hoarse, "Teacher's pet" one more time. Victoria Grace did her best to ignore him as she bowed her head to pray.

"Gracious Heavenly Father," Miss Cuthbert prayed, "we thank Thee for Thy many blessings. Bless these dear children as they seek to learn more about Thee today. Give them ears to hear Thy instruction, and may their minds be open to learning. Amen."

"Amen," the children echoed.

As she took her seat, Victoria Grace remained still and straight, hoping to be chosen for the morning recitation. Sure enough, Miss Cuthbert pointed at her and said, "Victoria Grace, would you please come to the front."

As she stood and approached the bench at the front of the classroom, Johnny's whisper grew a little louder. "Carrot top is teacher's pet. Carrot top is teacher's pet."

Victoria Grace's temper flared. *How dare he make fun of my red hair! How dare he call me carrot top! My hair is not orange like carrots.* Victoria Grace's mind raced. *My mother always says it is a lovely shade of auburn!*

"What was that you said, Mr. Gainsborough?" Miss Cuthbert looked at him with a stern face. "Please repeat it aloud in front of your classmates."

"Oh, I, um…" he stammered.

"You have disrupted the class far too many times this year to count," Miss Cuthbert said. "You will have to take your place in the corner once again."

With a troubled look on his face, Johnny rose from his seat and crossed the room to the corner in the back. There he stood with his nose against the wall. Victoria Grace gave a little shrug and came to the front of the room, where she joined Miss Cuthbert and several other students for the morning recitation.

"Open your *New England Primers*, children," Miss Cuthbert instructed, "and let us read aloud, one at a time. Victoria Grace, you may begin."

Speaking loud and clear, Victoria Grace read from the familiar book. Her voice seemed to echo across the classroom. She glanced up to see the younger children looking at her in awe.

After she finished reading, some of the other children read aloud from their readers. Victoria Grace loved this part of the day. Reading aloud was so much fun.

"You all did a lovely job this morning," Miss Cuthbert said with a smile. "You may take your seats." She glanced back to the corner where Johnny stood with his nose to the wall. "Mr. Gainsborough, you may take your seat as well."

He made his way back to the desk, and sat with a frown on his face. Victoria Grace tried not to pay any attention to him at all.

"We will now have our penmanship lesson," Mrs. Cuthbert said. "Children, get your hornbooks and practice your letters."

Victoria Grace reached for her hornbook—the wooden paddle with a piece of paper attached to it—and traced over the letters with her dry quill. Over and over she traced them, wishing she could dip her quill into the inkwell on her desk and write on real paper. Perhaps next time. Paper was hard to come by, so the children must practice this way for now.

A, a, a, a, B, b, b, b, C, c, c, c...on and on she traced the letters. Miss Cuthbert walked up and down the center aisle, looking over the children's shoulders as they worked. When she came to Victoria Grace, she gave her an admiring pat on the shoulder.

"Very nice, Victoria Grace," she said aloud. "You always trace your letters so carefully."

Victoria Grace smiled broadly, happy for the encouragement.

Just as the teacher turned to look at another student's work, Victoria Grace felt a little tug on her hair once again. She turned just as Johnny dipped the end of her braid into his inkwell. Victoria Grace let out a little squeal then clasped her hands over her mouth, embarrassed at her outburst.

"Miss McElyea, is there something you would like to say?" The teacher turned her way with a curious look on her face.

For a moment, Victoria Grace thought about tattling—then decided not to do it. The look of mischief in Johnny's eyes let her know he was only teasing. And, besides, he had already spent time in the corner this morning.

"I...I'm fine, Miss Cuthbert," she stammered, clutching her braid. Then, with a little giggle, she turned her attention to her penmanship once again.

Johnny whispered a quiet "Thank you," and she offered up a slight nod.

The rest of the morning passed quickly. Using their tiny slates, the children worked on arithmetic problems. Victoria Grace already knew how to add and subtract better than most of the other students, but Miss Cuthbert was working with many of the older children on their multiplication and division skills as well.

Victoria Grace concentrated on the figures in front of her. She wrote the answers on her slate, careful not to make any mistakes.

After awhile, Miss Cuthbert's voice rang out, capturing her attention. "I have an announcement to make," Miss Cuthbert said. "This afternoon, just after lunch and play-time, we will have our annual spelling bee. I can't wait to see who this year's winner will be."

Victoria Grace felt her heart swell with pride. She had won the spelling bee two years in a row. Surely she would win this year too.

As Miss Cuthbert rang the bell, dismissing the children for lunch, all of the boys and girls rose from their seats and lined up to walk outside. Victoria Grace usually enjoyed this part of the day best of all. Playing ring toss or competing in sack races after lunch was always a lot of fun…but not today.

No, not today, Victoria Grace thought. She wanted to remain behind to look over her list of words one last time. Perhaps, if she studied long enough and hard enough, she would win this year's spelling bee too.

"One day," she whispered, *"sick people will come to see me, and I will help them get better."*

DOC FINNEY

N Saturday morning, Victoria Grace sat down to breakfast with her parents and three brothers in the dining room of their large North Carolina home. As much as she loved school days, Saturdays were better still. On Saturdays she could spend hours and hours with her family.

"When are we leaving for town, Father?" she asked, as she finished her eggs and toast.

"Just as soon as Trevor and Todd help me prepare the wagon," he said, gesturing to her two older brothers. "It's mighty cold outside. We will need plenty of extra blankets." Her father then turned his attention back to Victoria Grace. "Are you in a hurry, darling?"

"Yes sir," she said, bouncing up and down in her seat, "I need to speak with Doc Finney right away."

"Doc Finney?" Her mother asked, giving her a curious look. "Why-ever would you need to speak to the doctor? Are you ill, child?"

"No, Mother." She tried not to giggle. "I want to ask Doc Finney if he will let me work alongside him in his office."

Her sixteen-year-old brother Trevor laughed long and loud. "You're not even twelve years old," he said. "Do you really think the doctor will hire you?"

"Perhaps not," she said as she crossed her arms and leaned back against the chair, "but I want to ask if he will allow me to watch him work and maybe assist him. Then one day I can become a doctor too."

"A doctor?" Fourteen-year-old Todd snorted. "You're a *girl*, silly."

"I know," she said as she sat up straight in her chair, "but girls can be doctors too."

"That's not possible," Trevor argued, "but even if you could, you're too little."

She gave her brother a stern look as she responded, "I'll be twelve in a few weeks. That's *plenty* old enough to work. Why, you started working in the hattery with Father when you were only eight years old."

"That's different. I'm a boy, and working in a hat shop is different from working alongside a doctor."

Victoria Grace couldn't help but let out a groan. She would never understand why boys got to do so much more than girls.

"I believe I know why she has her heart set on such a thing," Todd said with a laugh. "It's because of that spelling bee yesterday."

"Oh?" Her mother gave her a curious look. "Why didn't you tell us about the spelling bee, my darling? You're always so excited about it."

Victoria Grace hung her head in shame. She could hardly forgive herself for losing...and to Johnny Gainsborough, no less.

Todd chuckled. "The last word in the spelling bee— the one she missed—was *laceration*. She spelled it with an *s* instead of a *c*."

Victoria Grace continued to stare at the tablecloth for a moment before glancing up into her mother's caring eyes. "I knew it by heart," she explained. "I truly cannot believe I forgot it. I really wanted to win, but..." She drew in a deep breath, remembering the look of amusement on Johnny's face when she'd missed the word. She would never forget that look as long as she lived.

"Winning is certainly not the most important thing," her mother said, "and I'm sure you tried your best."

"Yes ma'am." Victoria Grace nodded, though she secretly still wished she had won. "But Miss Cuthbert asked me to stay after class so that she could tell me something in private. She thinks I'm very bright." Victoria Grace smiled, remembering. "In fact, she said I would make a fine teacher someday."

"A teacher!" Trevor said with a smile. "Now *that's* a job for a girl."

Immediately Victoria Grace's smile faded, and her lips curled downward in a pout. "But I *really* want to be a doctor, not a teacher."

"You heard what your brother said, darling," her father reminded her. "Only boys can be doctors."

"I know," she said, letting out a sigh, "but it's so unfair." She bit her lip, thinking about it. After a moment a smile rose to her lips, and she said, "But I can *help* Doc Finney, can't I? It would be simply wonderful!"

Her mother stood to clear the table. "When, exactly, would you do this? You are in school nearly every day, young lady."

"Yes, but school ends at two o'clock," she explained, "and I could work on Saturdays. I really, really want to do this, Mother. If Doc Finney is agreeable, may I? Please?"

Just then her baby brother Thomas let out a cry from his tiny cradle in the corner of the room. Victoria Grace rushed to him. She cradled him in her arms and nuzzled his soft hair against her cheek. She sang the first few words of a lullaby, and he calmed down right away.

"She *is* very good at caring for others," her mother said, looking at her father with a twinkle in her eye. "What harm would it do to let the child speak with the doctor?"

"No harm, I suppose." Her father rose from his chair and crossed the room to plant a kiss on Victoria Grace's forehead. "No harm at all."

Victoria Grace raced up the stairs to get dressed for her meeting with the doctor. She wanted to look her best. She carefully chose her green dress with the white lace around the neck because she liked the way the green matched her eyes. Then she went to work on her hair. She decided that tying it all back in a ribbon made her look a little older than the braid she usually wore to school. One quick look in the mirror and she knew she was ready.

Soon the whole family was loaded in the wagon and began their trip into town. Victoria Grace sat bundled in blankets, shivering against the cold air. Her teeth chattered as she spoke. "A…are we going to the Mercantile first?"

"Yes, Daughter," her mother said.

"C…can we v…visit with Doc Finney after that?"

"Yes, Daughter," both of her parents spoke in unison.

Everyone laughed, and then her mother added, "If we're not careful, we'll all need the doctor." She held the baby close, and with a shiver said, "It's freezing out here. I will be glad when spring arrives."

In no time at all the family pulled into town in their wagon. They rode past the blacksmith and beyond the coach maker's shop. On they went, beyond the silversmith and even McElyea's Hattery, the family hat shop.

"First things first," Mother said. "The Mercantile."

Minutes later they crossed the cobblestone streets on foot to enter the Mercantile. So many wonderful sights greeted them—fabrics, soaps, and candles lined the front counter. And there, off to the side, stood jars and jars of delectable candies: licorice, iced almonds, candied cherries, and her favorite, pralines.

"May we have some, Mother?" Victoria Grace asked, pointing to the pralines. "Please?"

"Perhaps," her mother said. "If you will help me with the rest of my shopping, I will consider it."

A short time later the family left the store with packages in their hands, and Victoria Grace held a bag of pralines for later. Father and the older boys began to walk in the direction of the hattery.

"Join us at the shop when you're finished at Doc Finney's," Father said.

Mother nodded, bundling the baby in his blankets, and together she and Victoria Grace made their way across the busy street to the doctor's office.

"Are you sure you want to do this, darling?" her mother asked as they approached the door.

"Quite sure."

They stepped inside the doctor's home, which also served as his office, and his wife greeted them with a broad smile. "Welcome, ladies," she exclaimed. "It's been a long time since I've laid eyes on you. You're a welcome sight. I do hope you aren't ill."

"No, we are all quite well. Thank you for asking." Mother gave her good friend a hug, and Mrs. Finney asked if she could hold baby Thomas. As soon as the youngster landed in her arms, he began to cry.

"I'm afraid I'm not very good with children," Mrs. Finney said as she tried to comfort the crying child. "The good doctor and I were never blessed with children of our own."

Mother nodded. "It's a child I've come to speak with you about," she explained, taking baby Thomas back in her arms. "My daughter, Victoria Grace, would like to visit with your husband, if you please. If he has time for a visit, that is."

Though Victoria Grace disliked being called a child, she did not interrupt.

"Indeed," Mrs. Finney said, with a curious look on her face. "He's with a patient now, but he should be done soon."

The ladies continued to chat as Victoria Grace looked around.

"How are things at the hattery?" Mrs. Finney asked.

"Quite good," Mother replied. "We have a new assortment of caps and cloaks. And you should see the new hats my husband, Lodwick, has fashioned. They're quite the style."

"I always say McElyea's Hattery has some of the prettiest hats and bonnets in town," Mrs. Finney said with a nod.

"Why, thank you," Mother replied. "Of course, hats are our specialty, but our dressmaking business has grown as well. My husband has hired another dressmaker to fill all of the orders."

As the two women began to talk about different styles of hats and dresses, Victoria Grace found her mind wandering. She glanced over at Doc Finney's framed certificate on the wall. "Pennsylvania College of Medicine, William Finney, Doctor of Medicine" it read. Perhaps one day she would have a certificate of her own.

"Victoria Grace McElyea, Doctor of Medicine," she whispered. A smile crept across her lips as she thought about the possibilities.

Just then the doctor entered the room with the patient at his side—an elderly man who walked with a cane. "Take care of yourself, Mr. Stonebridge," Doc Finney said, "and come back to see me in a few days if you're not feeling better."

As Mr. Stonebridge left, Victoria Grace turned her attention to the good doctor. With great passion in her voice, she explained her reason for coming. As she spoke, his lips curled up in a humorous smile. Afterwards he nodded his head and spoke with great seriousness.

"Why, I would be honored to have your assistance, Miss McElyea," he said. "What a wonderful idea. How often can I expect you?"

With her mother's help, they put together a schedule. Victoria Grace could come into town on Tuesdays and Thursdays after school and every other Saturday.

After their visit with Doc Finney, Victoria Grace and her mother joined the others at the hattery. Victoria Grace took charge of baby Thomas as the rest of the family worked. Her mind began to wander as she thought about helping the doctor.

"One day," she whispered, "sick people will come to see *me*, and I will help them get better."

With her heart overflowing, she turned her attention back to baby Thomas and sang him to sleep.

"Independence is what we need—to be free from the rule of the British."

WHISPERS OF WAR

*T*HE LAST SATURDAY IN MARCH, JUST AS Victoria Grace finished up at Doc Finney's office, her father and oldest brother Trevor came by to pick her up in the wagon after they closed the shop. As they approached, she overheard them talking.

"If something doesn't change soon, there will be a war. Mark my words," she heard her father say.

"Do you really think so?" Trevor asked. "Could we win a war against the British? They have superior weapons and plenty of fighting men. The colonists have little to compare with that."

"There are hundreds of colonists who would link arms and fight together for freedom," her father said. "Independence is what we need—to be free from the rule of the British." Just then he looked down from the wagon and noticed Victoria Grace standing there. "I'm sorry, Daughter," he said, jumping down to meet her. "I didn't see you coming."

"What were you and Trevor talking about, Father?" she asked. "What's all this about a war?"

He glanced back up at Trevor, who had a worried look on his face. Clearly, they did not want Victoria Grace to hear any more.

"Nothing for you to worry your pretty little head over," Father said. "Just man-talk."

Victoria Grace sighed. It seemed like everything was man-talk—except at Doc Finney's office. He treated her with great respect. Why, he had told her just today what a fine assistant she was.

"How was your day, Victoria Grace?" Trevor asked, obviously trying to change the direction of the conversation.

"Fine," she said. "Mrs. Jacobson came in with a case of poison ivy. Doc Finney instructed her to bathe in oatmeal when she got back home. In the meantime, I helped him apply a lotion to her red, bumpy spots." She smiled, remembering. "Oh, and Mrs. Brower brought in her twins boys because they had gotten into a scuffle and given each other a black eye—along with a few bumps and bruises all over."

Trevor laughed. "That's boys for you—always wrestling."

"Still," Victoria Grace said, "they should know better. They're eight years old. Fighting is no way to get what you want."

She couldn't help but notice Trevor and Father looking at one another as if they disagreed with her.

"Sometimes fighting is the *only* way to get what you want," Trevor said, his face growing stern.

"What do you mean?"

When he shook his head and wouldn't answer, she looked at her father. "What does he mean, Father? What's all this talk about fighting, anyway?"

As the wagon rolled along on the road out of town, her father turned to face her. "I suppose it's all right to tell you what's going on, Daughter," he explained. "You're a big girl now, and I know you will handle this news as best you can." His brow wrinkled a bit before he continued. "Times are very hard right now between the British and those of us who live in the American colonies. There's a rumor that we'll have no choice but to fight."

"Like the Brower twins?"

Her father sighed. "I guess you could put it like that. The British and the colonists were like brothers at one time. Some still believe we can be, but the relationship between the brothers has grown sour. One has turned on the other."

"Which one?" Victoria Grace asked.

An angry look crossed Trevor's face. "The British have turned their backs on us, and that's all there is to it."

Father nodded. "It's complicated, my darling, but the very people who set out to protect us won't give us the freedom to govern ourselves. Though we live here, in America, we're still being told what to do by men who live halfway across the world. And much of what they're telling us to do is unfair. We are being overtaxed, and we are not free to make our own laws and choose our own leaders."

"That doesn't seem fair," Victoria Grace said.

"Indeed, it is not," Father agreed, "and this unfairness has been going on far too long. Do you remember hearing about the Stamp Act?"

"Yes sir." She recited from memory the story Miss Cuthbert had taught them in school. "In 1765 King George the Third passed the Stamp Act."

"Do you remember why?" Father asked.

"Something about the French-Indian War?" she asked.

"Yes," Father explained, "to pay back money for the war, colonists were forced to pay taxes on many things like paper, newspapers, and the like."

"Even playing cards," Trevor added.

Victoria Grace shook her head. "That's awful."

"Truly," her father said, "but the Stamp Act was passed, regardless."

"It was?"

"Yes, and right away the colonists boycotted."

"Boycotted?" she asked. "What does that mean?"

"It means we wouldn't buy any British goods as long as we were being taxed unfairly," Trevor threw in. "Boycotting is kind of like twisting someone's arm."

"Oh, I see." Todd had twisted her arm once, years ago, and she didn't like it at all.

Trevor continued, "After awhile, King George did away with the unfair law, and we didn't have to pay the taxes any more."

"Well, that's good," Victoria Grace said. "Guess the colonists gave 'em a black eye that time around, eh?" She chuckled.

"I guess you could say that." Her father smiled. "But there were more skirmishes to come, just like I'll guess there will be more skirmishes between those Brower boys. Do you remember hearing about the Boston Tea Party?" he asked.

Victoria Grace's eyes grew wide. "Yes, Father. I remember. I thought you were talking about a *real* tea party at the time, but it wasn't, was it?"

"No." Father shook his head. "Back in December of 1773, several colonists dressed up like Mohawk Indians and went aboard three British ships."

"Dressed as Indians?" Victoria Grace asked. "I didn't know that part."

"Yes," Trevor said. "They busted open chests of tea and tossed the tea into the harbor."

"Sounds like they were angry," she said.

"Indeed." Father nodded. "Brothers do tend to get angry sometimes."

The wagon rolled down the country road, and Victoria Grace listened to the horses' hooves as they clip-clopped along, creating a rhythmic sound.

Father's soothing voice rose above the sound of the horses. "Since that time, things have only grown more tense between the colonists and the British. It's rather like those two Brower boys, growing more and more irritable with one another. Before long, someone is going to come out swinging."

"And the other will end up with an ugly black eye?" Victoria Grace asked.

"Perhaps." Her father turned his attention to the horses as they slowed to cross a narrow bridge over Morgan Creek. "It is our hope—our prayer—that we don't have to go to war. We pray that the British will come to their senses, but already, battles have taken place."

"They have?" Her eyes widened. "When? Where?"

"A couple of years ago there was a battle in West Virginia, in a place called Pleasant Point."

"But…" she looked at her father, for the first time afraid, "A real battle here in America? Do you think…" she swallowed back her fear as she continued, "do you

ELEANOR CLARK

think we could actually have fighting right here—in Surry County?"

Trevor's face tightened even more. "If the British cause trouble anywhere near here, I'll be the first to fight," he said.

"Now, calm down, Son," Father said, patting him on the back. "Let's not get all riled up. Before we do anything else, we will pray about the situation. We'll place it in God's hands and lean on the scripture that I've taught you since childhood." He smiled at both Trevor and Victoria Grace. "Can you recite it for me now?"

In unison, they said: *"Be strong and of a good courage; be not afraid, neither be thou dismayed: for the Lord thy God is with thee whithersoever thou goest*—Joshua, chapter one, verse nine."

"Very good," Father said with a smile as they turned the wagon toward their home. "I have a question." He gazed at them both, with a serious look in his eye. "Do you believe it? Do you believe the Lord will give you the courage to get through anything that might come your way?"

Trevor nodded right away, but Victoria Grace couldn't. A lump rose up in her throat, and for a minute she thought she might cry. If the British came—if a war started—she might not be so courageous. She might feel more like hiding under the bed or in the barn.

"Daughter, you are mighty quiet." Her father reached over to slip his arm around her shoulder. "Have we frightened you with all of this news?"

She nodded and then leaned her head on his shoulder. "It is frightening," she said, "but I know that God will protect us, just like the scripture says."

She thought about the Brower twins once again—with their bumps, bruises, and black eyes. They would recover quickly and soon be best friends again. Perhaps the same thing would happen between the colonists and the British. Victoria Grace looked up at her father with a determined smile. "I won't be terrified. I will be strong and courageous."

"Good girl." He placed a gentle kiss on her brow and turned his attention back to the team of horses. As they clip-clopped up the avenue toward the house, Victoria Grace thought about the words from the scripture once again. With God's help, she could be courageous—whatever came her way.

"Many things are happening around us, and I believe we can only be prepared to face them if we spend time reading the Word of God and asking the Lord to help us and give us courage."

FREEDOM AND COURAGE

*S*PRING CAME TO SURRY COUNTY THAT YEAR with a rush of color. Tiny flowers began to peek up through the bits of grass, covering the fields in yellow, pink, and purple. Victoria Grace stopped to pick some lovely golden daffodils on her way to school early one morning.

"What are you doing with those?" Adeline asked, joining her.

"I just think they're pretty," she explained as she lifted them up in the sunlight to get a closer look. "Perhaps I'll give them to Miss Cuthbert. She loves pretty things, and I love to see the smile on her face when she is delighted by something."

"I'll pick some too. We will give her a big bouquet." Adeline leaned down to find the nicest ones.

As Victoria Grace knelt beside her, she shared something she had just learned. "Doc Finney says some flowers can be used to make medicines. Did you know that?" When Adeline shook her head, Victoria Grace explained. "It's true. We called on Mr. Kensington just yesterday. He was suffering from a cold, so we made a tea with elderberry blossom. And last week, when Mrs. Dennison's baby was sick, we used catnip, flowers, and leaves to make a tea for her."

"That doesn't sound very tasty," Adeline said, plucking a large flower and gazing at it with pride.

"Medicinal herbs are often bitter," Victoria Grace said, "but they can work wonders. Did you know that moldy bread is good for a sore throat?"

Adeline looked over at her, amazed. "What? I don't believe it."

"It's true. Doc Finney takes the moldy part and soaks it in warm water. Then he drains it very well and gives it to his patients to use as a gargle. It works like a miracle on a sore throat."

With the bright yellow flowers clutched in her hand, Adeline gazed her way and sighed. "You're so smart, Victoria Grace," she said enviously. "I wish I was half as smart as you."

"And I wish I was half as pretty as you." With a giggle, Victoria Grace took her best friend by the arm, and they continued walking toward the school.

Moments later the school bell rang. Victoria Grace and Adeline presented their flowers to Miss Cuthbert, who took them with a smile and put them in a vase on her desk. "I do believe you children are spoiling me," she said with a wink. "Not that I'm complaining. I do love spring flowers."

As the schoolmarm took her place in front of the class, Victoria Grace sat up straight in her chair. After opening with prayer, Miss Cuthbert called out the date: "April 15, 1775." Then, as always, she began calling the children up to the front of the room for the morning recitation.

"Our reading today will come from the Bible," Miss Cuthbert said. "Rebecca, why don't you begin with the selection from Psalm 27:14."

Rebecca, a darling girl with blonde curls that bobbed up and down when she talked, read aloud in a cheerful voice: "*Wait on the LORD: be of good courage, and he shall strengthen thine heart: wait, I say, on the LORD.*"

"Very good," Miss Cuthbert said with an encouraging smile. "Now, who would like to read the next verse?"

Adeline's little brother Stephen raised his hand. "I will, Miss Cuthbert."

"Very good," she said. "Why don't you read the one from Joshua 10:25."

Stephen began to read…very slowly. "*And Joshua said unto them, Fear not, nor be dis… dis…*" He stared down at the Bible, and then looked up at the teacher for help.

"Dismayed," Miss Cuthbert said.

"*Dismayed,*" he echoed, "*be strong and of good courage: for thus shall the* LORD *do to all your enemies against whom ye fight.*"

"Thank you, Stephen. Adeline, would you like to read from Psalm 31:24, please?" Mrs. Cuthbert asked.

"Yes, ma'am" answered Adeline, who always seemed eager to read from the Bible. "*Be of good courage, and he shall strengthen your heart, all ye that hope in the* LORD."

Right away, Victoria Grace thought about all the talk she had heard lately about the possibility of war with the British. She raised her hand.

"Victoria Grace, do you have a question?" The teacher looked her way.

"Yes," she answered, her brows knit in concentration. "Reverend Compton read some of those verses last Sunday in church. I can't help but wonder if both of you have chosen these verses for a reason."

The teacher nodded and asked the students at the front of the classroom to be seated as she explained. "I can't speak for the reverend," she said, "but I have chosen them specifically. Many things are happening around us, and I believe we can only be prepared to face them if we spend time reading the Word of God and asking the Lord to help us and give us courage."

"My papa says there's going to be trouble," Johnny said, "and I think he's right."

"Your father is right," Todd added. "There's going to be trouble, all right."

"What kind of trouble?" one of the little girls asked. Her face grew pale as she said the next word. "Indians?"

"No," Miss Cuthbert assured her. "There haven't been any Indian uprisings in this area for many years, praise the Lord. I believe Johnny and Todd are referring to a possible problem between the colonists and the British."

All of the children began to talk at once, and Miss Cuthbert clapped her hands to get their attention. "Class, please!" After they settled down, she said, "We have no way of knowing what will happen for sure, but this much I do know. Here in the colonies, we believe very strongly in freedom. Many of your parents and grand-parents came from other places around the world to live in a place where they could worship freely. We don't ever want anyone to take that freedom away from us." A sad look came into her eyes all at once.

Victoria Grace raised her hand again. "My father says that freedom comes at a great cost. What does he mean by that?"

Miss Cuthbert nodded as she answered. "He means that sometimes people have to earn their freedom. They have to work for it. They have to…" her faced paled a little. "They have to fight for it."

"I'll fight," Johnny said, without even raising his hand, "if I have to." His eyes filled with anger. "I'll fight to the death!"

Victoria Grace thought about his words for a minute. If anyone knew how to pick a good fight, it was Johnny Gainsborough. Still, this wasn't *that* kind of fighting. Or was it?

Miss Cuthbert quieted the class once again. "We need to trust God for His will to be done and pray for courage to face what lies ahead."

Miss Cuthbert then turned her attention back to their lessons, reciting the list of spelling words in a crisp, clear voice.

Liberty

Courage

Persistence

Valor

Patriot

Revolution

"What does that last one mean, Miss Cuthbert?" one of the little girls asked.

"Ah, I wondered if someone might ask that question." Miss Cuthbert paused for a moment before continuing on. "A revolution, or a revolt, happens when people take a stand against someone—or something—they believe to be wrong. Some would say that the colonies are revolting against the British Empire, but I choose to think that we are just taking a stand for what is right."

Victoria Grace thought about her words. She didn't want to think of war—not now, not ever.

Miss Cuthbert continued to read through the list of words one at a time, giving their definitions. Then she encouraged the students to memorize them.

"We will now take the words and use them aloud in a few sentences," Miss Cuthbert instructed. "Can any of you think of a sentence or two using all of the words?"

Victoria Grace raised her hand.

"Yes, Victoria Grace?"

After standing, Victoria Grace spoke slowly and clearly, making sure she used every single word. "In order to obtain liberty, the colonists must have great courage, be persistent, and act with valor. We are patriots, and will win this revolution against the British." She smiled upon finishing.

"Very nice, indeed," Miss Cuthbert said.

As Victoria Grace sat, she thought about those words. *They'd been easy enough to put together in a sentence, but did she really believe what she had said? Would the Americans really have enough courage to face a huge army of British soldiers and fight for what they believed in? Perhaps only time would tell.*

After spelling, Miss Cuthbert instructed the children to work on their penmanship. As Victoria Grace opened her hornbook to trace her letters, she found herself tracing the verse from Joshua 1:9 instead. She loved this verse, which her Father shared so often: "*Be strong and of a good courage; be not afraid, neither be thou dismayed: for the* LORD *thy God is with thee whithersoever thou goest.*"

She looked up at Miss Cuthbert's desk, at the lovely yellow daffodils, and thought about how wonderful her life had always been, how carefree. Why, everything came easily to her—schoolwork, tending to the sick, caring for her little brother. Everything.

Victoria Grace leaned back in her chair, deep in thought. *If everything came easily to her, perhaps that meant, with God's help, she really could make it through something terribly difficult. Something like war.*

―――――∋●&――――

"A patriot is someone who loves
his country very much," Father
explained. "Someone who would
fight for his country, if need be."

―――――∋●&――――

THE BRITISH
ARE COMING!

APRIL 19, 1775

"THE BRITISH ARE COMING! THE BRITISH are coming!" Victoria Grace awoke to her brother's excited cry. "W...what?" she asked. Her heart began to pound right away, and beads of sweat popped up on her brow. Had the very thing she had feared most come to pass? Were British soldiers here? She sat up in bed and pushed back the covers, scrambling over the edge. "Are you sure? Really, truly sure?"

"Mr. Paul Revere has spread the word," Todd spoke with great zeal as he stood in the doorway of her room. "He has sent out the warning that the British are coming. They're already on their way."

She jumped from the bed and raced to her wardrobe to select a dress to wear. Almost at once, Mother joined her in the room. "Todd, please give me a hand with the baby. I want to speak to your sister."

After Todd left with baby Thomas, Mother turned to Victoria Grace with concern in her eyes. "I was afraid he would alarm you, child. I didn't want that."

"He did." She looked up into her mother's face. "He said the British are coming. Is that right?"

Mother slowly nodded. "Yes. I'm afraid that's right."

"What will happen, Mother?" Victoria Grace could hardly breathe as she thought about the possibilities. "Will there be a war?" Immediately her tears flowed. She didn't even try to stop them.

"Perhaps," Mother whispered, "though I can't be sure. But one thing is for sure—Father wishes to speak to the whole family right away. We will meet downstairs in the parlor." Her mother wiped away a tear. "Hurry, Daughter. No dawdling today."

"But what about school?"

Mother shook her head. "Not today. I'm sure school has been dismissed."

Victoria Grace dressed quickly and tied her long hair back with a ribbon, but her mind would not be stilled. She couldn't stop thinking about her brother's anxious cry: "The British are coming!"

What would happen? As she slipped on her shoes, she offered up a prayer, "Dear Lord, help us. Protect us. Amen."

Moments later the entire McElyea family met in the parlor. Father paced the room, finally stopping in front of the fireplace. "The British have painted us into a corner," he said, "and we have no choice but to fight."

"Oh, Father," Victoria Grace said as she raced to his side, "there must be some other way."

He shook his head, and then looked down at her with love in his eyes. "I will leave in the morning for Boston."

"Boston, Massachusetts?" Victoria Grace whispered. "Why so far away?"

"Many of the colonists are meeting there, even now. Much of the action will take place in that area," he explained, "at least, at first."

"I'm coming with you." Trevor stood, suddenly looking taller and older than he ever had.

"No, Son! Why, you're just a boy," Mother said with tears in her eyes.

"I'm a grown man." He spoke with a stern voice that Victoria Grace had never heard before. "And I must do what a man must do." He turned to Father, who offered up a nod of support.

"Trevor is seventeen," he explained, "and plenty old enough to join the ranks of other Patriots, if he so chooses."

"Patriots!" Victoria Grace exclaimed. "That was one of my spelling words. What does it mean again, Father?"

"A patriot is someone who loves his country very much," Father explained. "Someone who would fight for his country, if need be."

"Then I am truly a patriot," Trevor said, with determination in his voice. "I will fight for my country."

Father's voice softened a bit. "I would not encourage you to do so, Son, but I know that you have your heart set on joining us, and I will not stop you."

Trevor nodded. "When will we meet with the other men, Father?"

"We will meet at the schoolhouse in an hour," Father said, "and we will discuss our plan to join the regiments in the Boston area."

"Is everyone agreed that we should oppose the British?" Mother asked. "Or will we end up fighting our own neighbors and friends?"

Father shook his head. "Some in North Carolina will side with the British, I feel sure. I've heard people calling them "Loyalists" because they're loyal to Great Britain, but we will not bend our position. We will stand firm against tyranny."

"What's tyranny, Father?" Todd asked.

"I will do my best to explain it," Father said, looking into Todd's questioning eyes. "When someone is overly hard on someone else for no reason or for selfish reasons, that's called tyranny. The British have treated those of us in the American colonies with unnecessary harshness.

They've been cruel and unfair for their own selfish gain. Does that make sense?"

He nodded, but their mother still had concerns.

"I understand all of that," she said, "and I agree that something must be done. But I don't know how we can possibly win a war when the American colonies have no regular army." Mother fanned herself with the lovely hand-painted fan Father had purchased from Oriental traders. Victoria Grace could tell she was clearly worried.

Father tried to console her. "Each of the colonies will have its own militia," he explained. "They lack the training of the British forces, perhaps, and we certainly are not armed as well, but we all strongly believe in our right to liberty, and we will work together and get the job done."

Mother looked pale and worried. Victoria Grace noticed the tears in her eyes as she kissed the men.

Men. Victoria Grace thought about that word for a minute. Trevor really did look and act like a grown man, just as he had said. But did that mean he should go to war with the others?

As she thought about it, tears filled her eyes. She crossed the room, drawing close to her brother. "I don't want you to do this," she whispered, "but I understand that you must." She began to cry, and he swept her into his arms for a brotherly hug.

"Don't you fret, little sister," he said. "Pray for me. Pray for all of us."

"I will, indeed," Victoria Grace promised.

"We need to leave for the schoolhouse right away," Father said as he turned to his wife. "We will be back in a few hours, darling. If you don't mind, please go ahead and pack my trunk."

Shortly thereafter, many of the men in the county met at the schoolhouse to discuss their plans. Victoria Grace went to meet Adeline, and the two of them sneaked up to a window on the east side of the building to hear what they could.

"We are Americans," a stocky man by the name of Mr. Goodfellow spoke in a rousing voice. "Just like David stared down the mighty giant, Goliath, we must face our enemy head-on. We cannot allow fear to get in the way."

"It won't be that easy," one man cried out. "Many of our neighbors will side with the British Empire."

"And many will side with us," Mr. Goodfellow responded. "This is a challenge we must face."

At that time, one of the men in the room rose from his seat, and with a booming voice began to sing out a song Victoria Grace had never heard before. Within seconds, many of the others joined in. The walls of the schoolhouse trembled as the men, some fifty strong, sang together.

Come, join hand in hand, brave Americans all,
And rouse your bold hearts at fair Liberty's call;
No tyrannous acts shall suppress your just claim,
Or stain with dishonor America's name.

In Freedom we're born and in Freedom we'll live.
Our purses are ready. Steady, friends, steady;
Not as slaves, but as Freemen our money we'll give.

Our worthy forefathers, let's give them a cheer,
To climates unknown did courageously steer;
Thro' oceans to deserts for Freedom they came,
And dying, bequeath'd us their freedom and fame.

The tree their own hands had to Liberty rear'd,
They lived to behold growing strong and revered;
With transport they cried, Now our wishes we gain,
For our children shall gather the fruits of our pain.

Then join hand in hand, brave Americans all,
By uniting we stand, by dividing we fall;
In so righteous a cause let us hope to succeed,
For heaven approves of each generous deed.

The men's voices grew louder as they sang the chorus one last time. Victoria Grace and Adeline held hands as they listened in awe.

In Freedom we're born and in Freedom we'll live.
Our purses are ready. Steady, friends, steady;
Not as slaves, but as Freemen our money we'll give.

Victoria Grace and Adeline pulled away from the window and faced one another. Neither one spoke for a moment, both trying to soak it all in.

"I'm so scared," Adeline said, putting her hand to her mouth. "War is a terrible thing. My papa told me about the French-Indian war many years ago. His father was killed, and his brother too."

Victoria Grace gave a little shiver. "We must trust God," she said finally. "God will give us favor. I know He will."

"But everything will change." A tear drifted down Adeline's cheek. "Our menfolk will be gone, and the ladies will be left to fend for themselves."

Victoria Grace thought for a moment about that. If all of the men left, who would look after the others—to protect them and provide for them?

"Reverend Compton will stay," Victoria Grace said. "I know he will, and those of us who remain will meet together on Sundays for church. We will pray for those who have gone away to fight. Our prayers will be powerful."

"Yes, I feel sure of it," Adeline said, "but it just won't be the same without the rest of the men, will it?"

Victoria Grace thought about her friend's words for a minute, and then flew into action. "I have to go to town," she said suddenly.

"W…what?"

"I've got to talk to Doc Finney. There's something I need to ask him." At that, Victoria Grace turned on her heels and began to run toward town with Adeline close behind.

"I've been praying for courage," she
whispered, *"but I truly never believed
I would need it like I do now."*

BIG GIRL,
BIG DECISIONS

*V*ICTORIA GRACE RAN WITH ADELINE AT her side until she felt the blood pounding in her ears. They ran past the edge of the Yadkin River and then sprinted over the rickety bridge, not even bothering to look down onto the rushing waters below, as they usually did. They raced down the rocky road toward Doc Finney's place, determined to get there in record time. Victoria Grace had so many questions on her mind, but knew in her heart the good doctor could answer them all. Next to Father, he was the smartest man she knew.

When the girls got into town, the whole place was alive with activity. It seemed the news about the British had everyone stirred up. The Mercantile was filled to overflowing with people from around Surry County who had come to town to stock up on supplies. And the womenfolk all had tears in their eyes as they clung to the arms of their men.

"It's so sad," Victoria Grace whispered as she paused to take it all in.

"I know," Adeline said as her eyes filled with tears. She brushed them away and tried to put on her brave face. "But we must be strong and courageous, like Miss Cuthbert said."

Victoria Grace nodded and walked with determined steps. Still she couldn't help but wonder how many wives might lose their husbands in this war? And how many mothers might lose their sons? A shiver ran up her spine as she thought about it.

"Lord, please protect my brother and my father," she whispered. She didn't even want to think about what Mother would do if something happened to one of them.

On the girls ran, past the blacksmith shop, where old Mr. Cunningham worked in a frenzy to shoe horses. Past the hattery, where folks milled about, looking at the latest hat fashions. Beyond the front of Mr. Boyd's silversmith shop, where customers came and went, and past the boarding house, where Mrs. Kensington appeared to be feeding a large crowd of men.

Finally they arrived at the doctor's house and raced through the front door, not even bothering to knock. Adeline waited in the front room, but Victoria Grace ran directly into the office.

"Doc Finney, Doc Finney!" She spoke with tears streaming down her cheeks. "Have you heard what's happening?"

The elderly doctor turned away from the little boy he was tending to give her a "We will discuss this in a moment" look. She quietly slipped off to the edge of the room while he bandaged the youngster's scabby knee.

"There, son," he said as he finished. "Good as new. Would you care for a candy now?"

"Yes, please!" The little boy reached out his chubby fist to grab the piece of candy the doctor offered him. "Yummy!"

Minutes later Victoria Grace finally had the doctor's attention. "I'm sorry to have interrupted," she said with a sigh, "but what I've come to talk about is so awfully important."

"Yes, it is." He nodded, and for the first time she noticed the concern in his eyes. "You wanted to know if I have heard the news. Yes, dear girl. I have heard."

She clutched her hands to her chest, fearing his answer to her next question. "You're not leaving too, are you?"

He sat in the large wing-back chair and gestured for her to do the same. "I will stay here in Surry County unless I'm called away to care for the wounded elsewhere."

"You must stay," she pleaded. "You are the only doctor in the county. What would we do if you left?"

He nodded and gave her a serious look. "Victoria Grace, I must speak to you about something important." He gestured for his wife to enter the room. Then he closed the door so the patients waiting outside wouldn't hear. The good doctor turned to face Victoria Grace head-on. "You have been assisting me for… how long now?"

"A few months, sir."

"Yes. And a finer assistant I have never had." He glanced up at his wife, who reached to take his hand. "Next to my darling Cynthia, of course." His tone of voice grew more serious now. "But these coming months will be difficult, perhaps more difficult than any you have ever faced. I will need your help to care for the people of Surry County, as always, but it is likely that I will be calling on you to help me with those wounded from the war as well."

Victoria Grace's eyes grew large. "W…wounded?" she stammered. "I've never worked with wounded people before."

"Certainly you have." He gave her a reassuring smile. "Remember when little Matthew broke his arm swinging in that tree?"

"Yes sir."

"You helped me set it, did you not?"

"Well yes, but…" She remembered back to that day, how the youngster had cried out in pain. How her stomach had grown queasy as she assisted Doc Finney with the splint. "It was very hard."

"Indeed, but you've been through harder times than that. Remember when Mr. Jefferson cut his hand on the plow, nearly losing a finger in the process?"

She shuddered, remembering the sight of the blood. "Yes sir." It was by far the worst thing she had ever seen in her life, and she never cared to repeat it. She had cried all the way home, and had struggled to fall asleep that night.

"You were very brave that day," he said, "and I believe you will be even braver in the days to come."

"I've been praying for courage," she whispered, "but I truly never believed I would need it like I do now."

"You are stronger than you think," he said, "and time will prove that. As this war progresses, you will have the opportunity to either give in to the fear or to overcome it. I believe you will overcome it, to be sure."

He then went on to explain that the school year would probably be ending sooner than usual due to the current activities.

"When that happens," he said, "could you come into town three afternoons a week instead of two and possibly every Saturday?"

"Yes sir, I can as long as Mother agrees."

"I believe she will, and thank your mother for me, if you please," he said. "I know it will take great sacrifice on her part to allow you to come more often."

Victoria Grace bit her lip until it nearly bled as she thought about that. With Father and Trevor gone, Mother would need Victoria Grace's help around the house more than ever. But how could she balance her work at home and her work with Doc Finney?

"I'll do the very best I can to come," she assured him.

"I'm counting on it…and our fighting men are counting on it too."

As she and Adeline made the long walk home, Victoria Grace thought about Doc Finney's words. *I'm counting on it…and our fighting men are counting on it too.*

"They're all counting on me," she whispered.

Somehow, just knowing that gave her all the courage she needed.

There were tears in every eye as Father and Trevor rode away on horseback.

OFF TO WAR!

*T*HE DAY FATHER AND TREVOR LEFT WAS the hardest day of Victoria Grace's life. All day long she whispered the scripture he'd taught them from Joshua 1:9.

After kissing everyone good-bye, Father reached into his gun cabinet and pulled out a musket, which he handed to Trevor. The sight of Trevor holding a musket almost made Victoria Grace cry.

"Do promise me you will be careful with that," she whispered to him.

"I will." He nodded her way and gave her a little wink as he said, "I'm more grown up than you know."

"I know," she whispered in response.

Father then reached back into the cabinet and pointed to the knives and pistols. He looked at Todd and said in a rather stern voice, "Son, you are the man of the house now. I hope you never have to use these, but they are here, just in case."

Victoria Grace trembled as she heard his words. She couldn't imagine Todd picking up a weapon, not ever! Why in the world would Father say that?

Her father continued giving Todd instructions. "Your mother will handle much of the work at the shop, but she will occasionally need your assistance with deliveries. There will also be much to do around the farm."

Todd squared his shoulders and suddenly looked much older than his fourteen years. "I will do my best to protect and take care of the womenfolk, Father. Don't worry about the shop or the farm either."

Moments later the family stood on the front porch of the house saying good-bye to each other. There were tears in every eye as Father and Trevor rode away on horseback. Afterwards it was all Victoria Grace could do to make it back into the house and fall upon the sofa in the living room.

"Oh, Mother," she cried, "what will we do?"

Her mother sat next to her and reached to wrap an arm around her shoulders. "We will be strong and courageous," she whispered, "just like your father taught us to be."

Then her mother began to pray aloud: "Heavenly Father, we commit these men to Your work. Give them wisdom and skill. Guard their every footstep. Put a hedge of protection around them, and bring them home safely to us. These things we ask in Jesus' name. Amen."

Victoria Grace whispered a soft "Amen" along with her mother, and then looked into her eyes. How strong her mother seemed, in spite of everything.

Later that day, many of the people who remained in Surry County met together at the schoolhouse, which also served as the church. Reverend Compton led them in prayer for the men who had just left to fight for America's freedom. Many of the women had tears in their eyes, but Victoria Grace could see their determined looks as well. Mother looked the most determined of all. After the prayer service ended, her mother went to the reverend to shake his hand.

"I can't thank you enough," she said. "You will be a source of strength to us all while our men are away."

He gave her a warm smile and nodded. "God will be with the men, Mrs. McElyea. I feel sure of it."

The following weeks were very difficult, as Victoria Grace had expected. Every day Victoria Grace learned more details of Paul Revere's famous ride from village to village to warn the colonists that British soldiers had landed on American soil.

"One if by land, two if by sea!" Everyone in Surry County greeted one another with Mr. Revere's words of warning. Victoria Grace wasn't sure what they meant, exactly, so she asked her brother.

"Which was it, Todd?" she asked. "Did they arrive by land or by sea?"

"Paul Revere hung two lamps in the steeple of Old North Church," her brother explained, "to signal colonists that the British had arrived by water—the Charles River. Then he began his ride to warn people far and wide."

"Goodness gracious!" She could hardly imagine!

After hearing the stories, the people of North Carolina felt stronger than ever about fighting for their freedom.

With Father and Trevor away in Massachusetts, Todd did a good job taking care of the farm and helping out at the hattery whenever Mother needed him. Victoria Grace was busy herself, helping Mother with baby Thomas and working many hours for Doc Finney.

Her mother seemed to be the busiest of all. She kept the house and shop running smoothly and still had time to take care of all of them. Even though Mother was often weary from the workload, she never lost her courage. And neither did Victoria Grace.

After a while, Mother hired a woman named Martha Moore, whose husband had also gone off to war. Her duties included cooking and cleaning the house. Working for the McElyea's was an answer to prayer for Martha, since she needed a way to support herself while her husband was away. She had a broad smile and a laugh that just seemed to make everyone feel better. She was also a very hard worker, just like the Martha mentioned in the Bible.

Martha took over in the kitchen, but tending to the baby and working at the hattery still proved to be almost more than Mother could take at times.

"You look pale, Mother," Victoria Grace said after one particularly tiring day. "You've overworked yourself again."

"Possibly, but there's so much work to be done. Tending to the baby and working at the hattery is so exhausting."

Victoria Grace looked down at the ground. "If I didn't spend three days a week at Doc Finney's, I could help you more. I could take charge of Thomas for you. Would you like me to speak with the doctor? I could tell him that I could only come two days a week."

"No, darling," Mother protested, her expression growing serious. "Doc Finney needs you too much right now, and in time he might need you even more. I will manage. I have Martha to help me in the kitchen and with the house. And both you and Todd have been a great help to me, to be sure."

Victoria Grace smiled as she thought about Martha, who often sang aloud as she worked. Martha had been such a blessing to them all. Everyone loved her—and she loved everyone. She treated Mother just like a sister, even scolding her upon occasion when she overworked herself. Victoria Grace giggled as she thought about them being just like sisters. Mary and Martha were sisters in the Bible.

"I'll ask Martha to bring you breakfast in bed tomorrow," Victoria Grace said with a smile.

"Posh! Of course not. Why, I can come down to breakfast, and…" Mother put her hand over her mouth as she yawned.

"Mother, I insist. You go on to bed, and I'll go look for Martha now."

Without any further argument, her mother kissed her on the forehead and went to bed. Victoria Grace went in search of Martha. She found her in the drawing room, putting out the fire in the big fireplace.

"Martha?"

"Yes, Victoria Grace?"

"Mother isn't feeling well. Would it be possible to take her breakfast up on a tray in the morning?"

"Why, what's ailing your mother, dear?" Martha's eyes filled with concern. "She's not ill, is she?"

"No, not ill. Just worn out, I'm afraid."

"I tell you, that woman works harder than any person I've ever known. She works from sunup till sundown and never complains. Never." Martha shook her head and muttered, "And they say war is hard on the menfolk. Why, it's just plain hard on everyone."

Victoria Grace smiled. "You work just as hard, Martha," she said, "and I hate to ask you to do more, but

I'm sure Mother will feel better after a good night of rest and one of your wonderful meals."

"She surely will. I will see to that." Martha went on to list the foods she would make, and then turned off the oil lamps in the room as they left together.

"I hear tell General George Washington has been named our first commander in chief by the Continental Congress," Martha said with a wink.

"Commander in chief? What's that?" Victoria Grace gave her a curious stare.

"Why, that means he's the leader of the Continental Army and our country."

"Like a king?"

"Oh no, honey. General Washington was *chosen* by the good people of this country to represent them as their leader. It doesn't work like that with kings. Why, the King of England is only sitting on the throne right now because his father was king, and his father before him."

"How very odd," Victoria Grace said, thinking about that for a minute. "What if the people don't like the king? What if he isn't a very good ruler? Can they get another one?"

"No, Victoria Grace. I'm afraid not. Even really bad kings remain in power all of their lives."

"That sounds just awful."

"It is awful, and that is precisely why we hope to do things differently here in America. We want to place men in authority whom we can trust, men who are looking out for the country's best interests."

"I see."

Just before she headed up the stairs to go to bed, Victoria Grace looked at Martha with a smile. "I love having you here." She threw her arms around Martha's waist and gave her a friendly squeeze.

"Why, child, I love being here with you too. You're such a delight, and I'm so proud of you. I don't know that I've told you before, but I am. You're such a big help to your mother, and the work you do with the doctor in town is a real blessing to so many."

Victoria Grace tried to smile, but suddenly she felt rather sad.

"Have I said something to upset you, child?"

"Oh, no ma'am. It's just that…" she forced back the lump in her throat, "I miss Father, and I worry about him sometimes. I try hard not to, but when the weeks go by and no letters come, I can't help but worry."

"I know it's hard," Martha said. "I miss my dear husband very much. God bless him."

"Could you tell me more about your husband?" Victoria Grace asked, realizing that she didn't know much about him.

"Of course." Martha's smile widened, and her eyes sparkled with delight. "His name is Bradford Moore.

And he's the most handsome man you would ever meet, if I do say so myself."

Victoria Grace couldn't help but giggle.

Martha went on to describe him, smiling all the while. "I do love that man so much," she said. "I thank God for him every single day, and I pray for his protection as the war rages on. I understand that he made it through the Bunker Hill battle in Boston, Massachusetts, without a scratch. God bless him."

"Boston, Massachusetts!" Victoria Grace exclaimed, "That's where Trevor and Father went. Do you think they fought in the battle as well?"

"Why, I don't know. But Bradford told me about the battle. Would you like to hear about it?"

"I sure would," Victoria Grace answered, her eyes widening in anticipation.

Martha's eyes lit up with excitement as she stood and shouted, "Don't shoot till you see the whites of their eyes!"

"What in the world do you mean?" Victoria Grace asked.

Martha chuckled. "Why, I'm just quoting something Bradford wrote about in one of his letters. At the Battle of Bunker Hill, the Patriots didn't have enough bullets or gunpowder, so they were given the order not to shoot until they saw the whites of their enemy's eyes. That way they wouldn't waste any ammunition—every shot would find its mark."

"Oh, I see," Victoria Grace said. Martha told the story with such zeal that Victoria Grace could almost see it all in her mind.

"My Bradford is a good shot, so I know he didn't waste any ammunition," Martha bragged. Her expression suddenly became quite serious. "Still I must continue to pray for him that the good Lord will protect him."

"Will you pray for my father and brother too?" Victoria Grace asked. "Please?"

"Why, darling girl, I do! I pray for your father and brother every morning before my feet hit the floor."

Victoria Grace reached around Martha's waist one more time to give her another hug. "Bless you, Martha! God bless you."

As she pounced up the stairs, she thought about Martha's prayers. Most of the fighting men probably had wives and families back home to pray for them, but perhaps others did not. Victoria Grace decided right away that she would pray for all of the soldiers each night before going to bed.

With that in mind, she entered her bedroom, dressed for bed, and then dropped to her knees at her bedside. With her forehead leaning against the mattress, she began to pray for her father and brother and all of the men who had gone off to battle. Then she prayed that all the womenfolk would have strength while their loved ones were away. Finally she ended her prayer: "Lord, please give an extra-special blessing to Martha, and bring her husband back home to her safe and sound. Amen."

As she crawled into bed, Victoria Grace thought about how tired she was. It was hard working for Doc Finney and helping Mother out as much as she could, but God was giving her the strength and courage she needed. Right now, tired or not, she felt as if she could do just about anything.

"Our parents want us to grow up
in a country where we can vote
for our leaders and where we are
free to worship as we choose."

TRUE PATRIOTS

*T*HE SUMMER PASSED WITH ONLY A FEW letters from Father and Trevor. When school started in September, Victoria Grace wondered how she might be able to work with Doc Finney, help her mother with Thomas (who was walking now and getting into everything), *and* go to school. Surely the combination would make her quite weary.

Still she couldn't imagine *not* going. She loved school and wanted to learn all she could, especially now that the doctor had taken her under his wing and taught her so much about caring for the sick. It seemed that the more she learned the more she wanted to learn. Doc Finney had taken to calling her "Little Sponge" because she seemed to soak up the things he taught her with no problem at all.

On the first day of school, Adeline's little brother Stephen followed along behind the girls as they walked to the one-room schoolhouse together. He marched with steady steps, acting very much like a wooden toy soldier. His eyes remained fixed on the road ahead.

Victoria Grace shifted her lunch pail from one arm to the other, turning back to look at him. Then she asked, "What are you doing, Stephen?"

His voice rang out. "I've joined the Continental Army." He continued to take steps one after the other. He moved a bit to the right to avoid a puddle in the dirt road.

"What? How could you…?" Adeline asked, looking stunned.

"Why, you're too young!" Victoria Grace added. "It's impossible!"

"I'm pretending," he said as he stopped and gazed into his sister's eyes. "Father is in the Continental, and I would be too if I were old enough."

"Thank goodness you are *not* old enough," Adeline scolded. "Honestly, it is enough that Father has gone away to fight, but if you…" Tears came to her eyes and she pushed them away. "I don't know what Mother and I would do if you went away too. There will be plenty of time to talk about armies and wars and such when you are older."

Stephen shrugged and took off in the direction of the schoolhouse, where he joined his friends for a game of marbles.

One of the little girls approached Victoria Grace and Adeline with a sad look on her face. "Did you hear the news?" she asked.

"News? No, I don't believe so." Victoria Grace's heart skipped a beat. These days, whenever someone mentioned "news" it was often not good. "What has happened?"

"Johnny Gainsborough has gone off and joined the Continental Army," the girl explained.

"W…what? That's not possible. He's just fourteen. The same age as Todd!"

"I know," the girl said, "but he left with only a note to his mother. He said he was going to find his father and fight for the cause of freedom."

"I can hardly believe it." Victoria Grace sat on the schoolhouse steps and felt her eyes fill with tears. "He's been so mean to me, but I would feel awful if anything happened to him."

"I know," Adeline agreed. "I would too."

"He's a pesky boy," said Victoria Grace, "but he's just that—a boy, not a man. Only the men need to be fighting."

"Mother says we've lost some of the menfolk from Surry County already," Adeline said. "Did you hear about Mr. Devonshire—the man who runs the Mercantile?"

"Yes." Victoria Grace nodded slowly.

"It's so hard to believe. He was wounded in battle and infection set in. He died. Can you imagine?"

"Yes, actually." Victoria Grace nodded. "Infection is a terrible problem if wounds aren't cared for properly. Just the other day Doc Finney and I worked on a patient with a terrible infection in his leg. Doc Finney managed to get it under control just in time."

"It's all so awful," Adeline said with a shiver. "And poor Mrs. Devonshire…left all alone to work at the Mercantile and raise the little ones. She must be so sad."

"She is," Victoria Grace said. "I stopped in the store on Saturday when I left Doc Finney's. Several of the women were there with her, and they were all crying." Her mind drifted to the Devonshire children, Jacob and Lilly. She wondered if they would return to school or stay home with their mother.

"War changes everything," Adeline said, her eyes filling with tears, "everything. I don't like hearing about people dying, no matter what the cause. And when I put my head on my pillow at night, sometimes I am afraid."

"I know." Victoria Grace wrapped her arm around her friend's shoulder. "I know what it is to be afraid. I look forward to every letter from Father and Trevor so that I can know they're safe." She shook her head and forced back the lump in her throat. "But you know what?"

"What?"

"I know that Father was right when he said some things are worth fighting for. If we don't take a stand for what is right, will our children? And their children?"

"What do you mean?" Adeline dried her eyes and gave her a curious gaze.

"I mean, our parents are setting an example for us to follow. They want us to know that when you believe very strongly in something, you need to take a stand for it. Perhaps when we are grown, we will be asked to take a stand for something too."

"Oh, I hope not." Adeline gave a little shiver.

"I hope not either," Victoria Grace agreed, "but watching Father and Trevor head off to war has made me stronger and more courageous. I believe in our country's freedom now more than ever."

"You do?"

"I do. I am a true patriot. I want to be able to live in a land that is free," she explained. "Mother told me that her parents came to America for that very reason—to be free. They brought her to the American colonies all the way from Europe when she was just a little girl. Mother said that freedom can be lost very easily and that we must always protect it and stand for what is right, no matter how difficult." Victoria Grace squared her shoulders and looked around the school yard. "Our parents want us to grow up in a country where we can vote for our leaders and where we are free to worship as we choose."

"My goodness, you've been studying up on this," Adeline said. "Didn't you take a summer break at all, Victoria Grace, or are you *always* learning?"

The two girls giggled, which was quite a relief after the heavy conversation. Just then Miss Cuthbert rang the morning bell, ushering the children into the classroom. They took their places at their desks, and the teacher led them in a morning prayer.

"Heavenly Father, we ask Thy blessings on these Thy children. Guard their hearts and minds. Protect them, I pray. Be with their fathers, brothers, and friends who are fighting even now. Place a hedge of protection around them. Guard them on every side. And Father…" here her voice grew stronger, "please make us victorious in battle. Give us the courage of Daniel as he faced the lion's den. Strengthen us from the inside out. This we ask in the name of Thy Son, Jesus. Amen."

The children all echoed an "Amen" and then took their seats.

Miss Cuthbert looked them over with a smile. "We have a few new students this year," she noted, "and I believe a few have moved on as well."

Adeline raised her hand. "Miss Cuthbert?"

"Yes, dear?"

Adeline stood to her feet to speak. "Johnny Gainsborough has run off to join the Continental Army. We need to pray for him."

"Indeed. I'd heard as much." Miss Cuthbert shook her head. "We will pray for his protection. Join me, students." She bowed her head and prayed a lengthy prayer for Johnny's safety.

Then class began. After a few minutes, Victoria Grace settled into the routine. Starting a new year at school was always a bit difficult, but this year the students seemed to be more united—closer to one another. Perhaps the war had somehow brought them together.

As she sat in her desk with little Stephen behind her, she couldn't help but think of Johnny. She almost missed his teasing and taunting. For just a moment she wished he would reach over and grab her braid or tease her about her hair. A lump rose in her throat as she thought about him out on the battlefield. He might be a nuisance, but even a nuisance shouldn't have to fight a grown man's war.

With a prayer on her lips, she turned her attention back to her schoolwork.

*There, with her friends and
family gathered all around, she
renewed her commitment to follow
Christ all the days of her life.*

RENEWED
COMMITMENT

*T*HE WARM DAYS OF EARLY FALL TURNED chilly in no time at all. Before Victoria Grace knew it, November had arrived. The leaves on the trees changed colors in much the same way that so many other changes had come to Surry County. By now the womenfolk were doing a fair job of caring for their families and the crops, though they all longed for the war to end soon so that their men could return home again. Todd continued on as the man of the house, helping around the farm, and assisting Mother at the hattery. Victoria Grace carried on as well, assisting the doctor and helping her mother at home.

On the first Saturday in November, Mother asked Todd to bring the wagon around to take the family into town.

"If you can spare a few hours away from Doc Finney's, I could use your help at the store," Mother said to Victoria Grace. "Mrs. Oberdeen, the newest dressmaker, has more orders than she can fill and needs our help. We also need to display some of the new hats that have been made."

"Certainly, Mother."

They bundled up in blankets to make the trip to town in the wagon. Todd steered the team of horses along the winding road. Their feet clippity-clopped in steady rhythm, leaving trails of dust behind.

The family arrived to find the place rather quiet for a Saturday.

"With so many of the men away, this whole town seems vacant, doesn't it?" Mother observed.

"It does, at that," Todd agreed.

As they approached the hattery, Victoria Grace tried not to think about how much she missed her father and Trevor. And as she worked alongside her mother all morning long, she tried to quiet the ache in her heart. She did her best to think on happier things—like the lovely blue dress Mrs. Oberdeen was sewing for one of their well-to-do customers and the fashionable hats they were placing on the shelves.

After working with her mother for several hours, Victoria Grace asked if she could go to Doc Finney's for a little while.

"Of course, darling," her mother said. "Just return before the sun begins to go down. We need to make the journey home before dark."

"Yes ma'am."

She walked across the quiet street in the direction of Doc's house. Along the way, she passed by the Mercantile and stopped in for just a moment to say hello to Mrs. Devonshire and the children. The usually happy-go-lucky woman wore the saddest expression Victoria Grace had ever seen.

Mrs. Devonshire visited at length with Reverend Compton, who read to her from the Bible, and even offered to pray. Victoria Grace listened quietly as the man's rich voice read the familiar scriptures. Somehow, hearing the verses he read just made her feel better.

When the grown-ups were almost finished talking, Victoria Grace politely asked Mrs. Devonshire if Jacob and Lilly were nearby. The two youngsters came down from their little apartment above the store and embraced Victoria Grace with tears in their eyes.

"I miss my papa so much," Lilly said, with tears streaming down her face.

"I know, darling," said Victoria Grace. Her heart ached, just thinking about it. *What would she do if her own father....* No, she wouldn't think about it. She couldn't.

"One thing we can do is to continue to meet together on Sundays," the kindly reverend said as he was walking to the door. "Tomorrow morning I will share a special message about someone else who gave His life for the cause of freedom."

For the rest of the day, Victoria Grace pondered the reverend's words. Someone else had died for the cause of freedom. Could it be...? Was he talking about...? Yes, surely she already knew what Reverend Compton's sermon would be about, though she could hardly wait to hear it.

The next morning she awoke extra early and dressed for church as quickly as she could.

"My goodness, you're up before the roosters," Mother said, as they met for breakfast.

"Yes ma'am. I am." Victoria Grace helped feed Thomas, and then waited anxiously for Todd to bring the wagon around so they could leave for church.

When they arrived for church, people were still outside visiting. Mother went at once to Mrs. Devonshire and wrapped her arms around her, offering her words of encouragement. Victoria Grace spoke briefly to Adeline and nodded at many of her friends, but went inside quickly to take her seat.

"Why, you're here bright and early, Victoria Grace," Reverend Compton said as he passed her way.

"Yes sir." She smiled in his direction.

He paused to give her a pat on the shoulder along with a chuckle. "Wondering about my message this morning?" he asked.

She gave a little giggle. "I am. You made me curious yesterday."

"Ah, I see." He gave her a little wink and started to move on to visit with the others. "I do hope you enjoy it."

"I'm sure I will," she replied.

Minutes later the service began and everyone joined together in the singing of hymns. This was Victoria Grace's favorite part. She loved singing hymns to God, and enjoyed hearing others sing their praises as well. As they sang, *A Mighty Fortress is Our God*, she couldn't help but think about God being their fortress and strength during this time of war.

After some hearty singing and an intense prayer for the safety of the fighting men, Reverend Compton's sermon began. He spoke of someone quite wonderful who had given His life so that all men and women could be set free. That man's name is Jesus Christ, the Son of God.

"I knew it!" Victoria Grace whispered. She had known the message would be about Jesus. She had heard the story from the Bible many times before, but always loved hearing it again. Her heart swelled with joy at the truth that Jesus had given His life on the cross so that *she* could be free from sin and death.

After the message, Reverend Compton asked if anyone in the congregation would like to experience the freedom that comes from knowing and following Jesus Christ. Many in the congregation, including Adeline's little brother, went forward to make a commitment to the Lord.

Victoria Grace silently thanked God for Reverend Compton's sermon. She prayed that everyone in the congregation would experience the freedom she already knew as a believer.

Then, with great joy in her heart, Victoria Grace rose to her feet to move to the front. There, with her friends and family gathered all around, she renewed her commitment to follow Christ all the days of her life. Truly, He would give her the courage to make it through any challenges she might face.

—⟫●⟪—

*The place was full of wounded soldiers,
and in uniforms she did not recognize.
Many were badly wounded, and the
sight of it made her stomach sick.*

—⟫●⟪—

TENDING THE WOUNDED

N SPITE OF THE WONDERFUL SERVICES AT church, Christmas in Surry County was still a little sad that year. With so many loved ones away fighting in the war, nothing felt quite the same. The frigid cold that set in made things even more difficult, but the McElyea family still tried to have a festive Christmas in spite of it all.

"We must remember," Mother said, "that Christmas is still Christmas, in good times and bad. Your father would want us to celebrate the birth of the Christ-child, even during the war."

Victoria Grace tried hard to agree. She missed Father and Trevor more than ever, but enjoyed having Martha with them. Her mother and Martha made the most wonderful Christmas dinner, and Victoria Grace learned how to make plum pudding.

After Christmas, she spent the next few weeks helping her mother with Thomas and making sure that Todd didn't overwork himself.

A blanket of snow covered the McElyea farm for much of January, leaving Victoria Grace feeling cold inside and out. With such harsh weather, school was dismissed for several weeks in a row. Victoria Grace missed seeing Adeline and her other school friends, but she took advantage of her time at home, spending time with her mother and playing with Thomas.

At the end of February, just as the snow began to melt, a courier on horseback arrived at the McElyea home with a letter in his hand. "For Miss Victoria Grace," he announced.

She quickly broke the wax seal, read the letter, and then turned to her mother. "Doc Finney has sent for me," she said, "and I must go right away. There has been a battle nearby, and the wounded have been brought to Doc Finney to be tended to."

Her mother nodded, though her face paled a bit. "I'll get Todd to take you to town, so you won't have to make the journey on foot. You will arrive faster that way."

As Victoria Grace turned from the room, her mother called out her name. "Victoria Grace?"

"Yes ma'am?" She turned back toward her mother.

"I am very proud of you." Her mother's eyes filled with tears. "Over these past few months you have grown into a remarkable young woman."

Victoria Grace squared her shoulders and stood as tall as she could. "Thank you, Mother. I believe I have grown up, to be sure. And though this isn't the way I would have chosen to grow up, now that I'm thirteen, I *feel* older."

"I am sorry we didn't have much of a birthday celebration this year." Mother shrugged.

"It doesn't matter," Victoria Grace said. "We can celebrate next year, when I turn fourteen. Surely the war will be over by then."

Minutes later Todd helped her climb aboard the wagon for the trip into town.

"I'll wait with you in town," he said, as the horses clip-clopped along.

"You needn't do that, Todd," she said. "Likely, I will be at Doc Finney's for quite some time.

"I'll wait," he repeated, "there's plenty of work to be done at the hattery, after all."

As the wagon drew closer to town, Victoria Grace noticed more people out on the streets than before. Surely word had gotten out about the battle nearby and folks were concerned that their loved ones might be among the wounded.

Todd eased the horses through the crowd of people until they finally arrived in front of Doc Finney's place.

Victoria Grace hopped down from the wagon and entered Doc's house, looking around in amazement. The place was full of wounded soldiers, and in uniforms she did not recognize. Many were badly wounded, and the sight of it made her stomach sick.

She squeezed her eyes shut for a moment, trying to block it out of her mind. It was all too horrible. "I'm not sure I can do this," she said aloud.

"You have to, Victoria Grace," Doc Finney said as he stood by her side. His strong words brought her back to her senses. She looked up at him in despair.

"Oh, Doc. I'm not sure I am prepared for this. I don't know if I can do it."

"You can," he said, looking directly into her eyes. "Remember all those months ago when you told me that you were praying for courage? Remember that verse you shared with me?"

"Yes." She whispered it again, just to remind herself.

"God will answer your prayers," Doc said. "He will make you strong and courageous. I believe that you are braver than you think, and I know you can do this. I need your help, and I need it badly. There's been a terrible battle here in North Carolina, at Moore's Creek."

"Moore's Creek?" Her heart quickened. *A battle so close to home?*

"The Patriots have triumphed in that battle. Praise God," Doc Finney said. "Only two of our men were hurt, but many enemy soldiers have been wounded. I'm sure you've noticed the uniforms of the Redcoats."

"Yes sir."

"There are too many injuries for the doctors on the field to tend to—so some of the wounded from the British Army have been transported to us for care."

Victoria Grace followed along behind him into his office, where six or seven patients lay about on stretchers. Like those in the outer office, they wore red coats, and she knew at once they were enemy soldiers. "Oh, Doc!" she whispered. "Must we care for them, really?"

"We must. They have been captured by our men—taken prisoner. We will treat them as well as our own, as God would want."

"Yes sir." She nodded, and promised herself she would do her best.

The good doctor gestured toward one young man, a Patriot soldier, who lay very still. He didn't move at all at first, but she finally saw him take a tiny breath.

"What's wrong with that one, Doc?" she whispered.

Doc Finney shook his head. "I'm afraid it's probably too late for that one. It's a real shame. He's so young, and he is one of our own, after all. I believe you know him."

She walked over and looked into the boy's eyes, and then realized who she was looking at.

"Johnny." She whispered his name, and then reached to clutch his hand. "Johnny Gainsborough."

His eyes fluttered open slightly and he looked her way. "V...Vic...toria." His eyes closed again, and then she heard him whisper, "I...I'm s...so glad you're here."

"Johnny, you're going to be fine." She spoke in her most reassuring voice. "Doc Finney is here and he's going to help you." She looked up into the doctor's eyes, but he only shook his head.

Doc Finney took her by the arm and led her to the side of the room. "He's badly wounded, Victoria Grace. He's been...well, there's no easy way to say it...he's received a bayonet wound to the chest, and infection has already set in. His fever is raging."

"Surely there is something you can do!" Victoria Grace exclaimed. "Clean the wound. I will help you. I can do that."

"You don't understand." His whisper grew louder. "Gangrene has already set into the wound. Once that happens..."

"I know," she said, "but there's got to be something..."

"We can only make him comfortable until his parents arrive." Doc Finney patted her on the back. "I've done all I can, but we must leave him in God's hands now, child."

Victoria Grace began to cry at once, and the doctor allowed her to grieve. But after a few minutes, he told her to dry her eyes and head back over to comfort Johnny. She swallowed back the fear and did so.

"Johnny, I'm here." She squeezed his hand, and he gave hers a little squeeze in response.

"I... I'm glad," he whispered. "W...where is my mother?"

"She is on her way. She should be here shortly."

"I... I told you I would fight," he stammered. "Remember?"

"I remember."

"We'll stop those Redcoats if it's the last thing we do."

"Yes, Johnny. We will." She tried not to let the tears fall as she gripped his hand. "You're very brave…the bravest boy I know." A lump filled her throat as she thought about those words. He was brave because he had been willing to give his life for the cause of freedom.

"I...I'm sorry for t...teasing you," Johnny stammered.

She felt her cheeks flush in embarrassment. "It's all right. You're forgiven."

At that moment Mrs. Gainsborough entered the room with her husband at her side. "Where is my boy?" she cried out. "Where's my Johnny?"

Doc Finney rushed her to Johnny's side, and she began to weep aloud. "Oh, my son, my son!"

Victoria Grace backed away into a corner and began to sob as well. "Why, Lord?" she cried out. "Why Johnny? He's just a boy, not a man."

She didn't get to grieve long before Doc Finney came to ask for her assistance. "We have several in need of urgent care. Come with me, please."

He turned to help an older man, a second wounded Patriot soldier. The fellow cried out in pain, clutching his arm. The doctor examined the arm carefully, and then told Victoria Grace to get the antiseptic, along with a needle and thread.

"This wound will need care right away," he said. "Do you think you can stitch him up, Victoria Grace?"

"B…by myself?"

"Yes. I must help this other fellow immediately." He gestured to one of the Redcoats, a man about her father's age. "He has a wound to the stomach, and I will need to operate."

"Operate? But who will help you if I'm here, caring for the others?"

"My wife will help with the operation."

"I see." Victoria Grace nodded, but was still a little unsure.

Doc Finney gave her further instructions. "When you're done stitching up the Patriot soldier's arm wound, please see about the British soldier in the front room, the one with the head injury. He will need stitches as well, no doubt. And please keep a close eye on young Johnny, of course."

"Johnny Gainsborough," Victoria Grace whispered. "He's my friend."

The next several hours were spent tending to one wounded soldier after another. As she cared for the British soldier with the head injury, the talkative fellow spoke about his family back home in England. He had a wife and three young children.

"I wonder if I will ever see them again," he said with a faraway look in his eyes.

Victoria Grace couldn't speak past the lump in her throat. Why, this man was very much like her own father in many ways...except one, of course. He was a Redcoat. Her father was a Patriot. Still they seemed to have much in common.

On and on she worked, tending to one man after another. Just about the time Victoria Grace thought she would collapse from exhaustion, she turned to find her brother standing at her side, ready to help.

"Todd, you've come!"

"I have." He handed one of the men a cup of water. "I am very proud of you for the work you are doing, and I want to help. Though..." He looked around the room at the Redcoats and shook his head. "It will be a difficult thing to care for the enemy soldiers, I must confess."

"Yes, I know what you mean," Victoria Grace said. "Though not as hard as you might imagine." She thought about the British soldier and the stories he'd told of his three children.

"I do believe Father would expect us to care for them just as we would care for our own," Todd was quick to admit. "I don't want to let him down."

"Oh, Todd!" She put her arms around his waist and hugged him tight. "I'm so glad you are here with me, and I know that Father would be proud too."

"Thanks," Todd's faced beamed with the compliment, "and I must say that you have grown much these past few months. You are not the same little sister I used to tease. Oh, you've always had plenty of pluck, to be sure. But now there's a strength in you that I didn't see before."

Brother and sister worked side by side until the sunlight outside the window eventually faded away and night skies took over. During those hours, Victoria Grace saw things she had never seen before. On one occasion, she felt as if she might be sick. She turned to run from the room, catching her breath in the nearby hallway. As she did, she heard Johnny's mother cry out.

"No!" she hollered. "Please, Lord. No!"

Victoria Grace raced into the room, where she saw Mrs. Gainsborough leaning down over Johnny's lifeless body. Mr. Gainsborough reached to gently pull his wife away, but she would not move.

"My boy, my boy," she cried out over and over again.

Victoria Grace stood in stunned silence at the edge of the room. Then, quite suddenly, she began to feel very dizzy. Everything around her began to spin. Her eyes fluttered closed, and just a second later everything went black.

"But I think it takes almost as much courage to stay home and go on with the everyday things like you and your mother are doing."

COURAGEOUS
WOMEN

ICTORIA GRACE AWOKE IN A FOG TO THE powerful aroma of smelling salts. Her head felt heavy and strange. "W…what happened?"

"You're fine, child." Doc Finney stood over her, looking down with concern in his eyes. "You just fainted."

She heard his words, but they sounded rather hollow—like an echo. For a few seconds, Victoria Grace felt as if she were in a lake, swimming, swimming, swimming. She blinked her eyes and looked around, trying to remember what had happened to her. Ah yes. She had just received the news. Johnny Gainsborough was…

She shook her head, trying not to think about it. "M… may I sit up?"

"Slowly, child. Slowly." He helped her sit up against the wall.

"You gave us quite a scare." Todd looked down at her with a wrinkled brow. "I've never seen anyone faint before."

Victoria Grace leaned her aching head back against the wall. "I'm sorry I alarmed you, especially when there are so many others who really need our help."

"Most of the men are sleeping now," Todd assured her. "We just want to make sure you are all right."

"I am." She closed her eyes and drew in a deep breath. "Truly. Don't worry about me."

"It's hard not to worry about you," he teased with a smile.

He sat beside her on the floor and held her hand. For a few minutes, neither of them said anything. Then, finally, Victoria Grace began to cry. She cried because of Johnny. She cried because she missed her father and brother. She cried thinking about the young British soldier, wondering if he would ever see his family again. And she cried because the war seemed to be taking every ounce of strength out of her.

"Sometimes I wonder if I can go on," she whispered at last. "I'm so weary."

"I get like that sometimes too," Todd said, "but then I remember the verse Father taught us."

Victoria Grace couldn't help but smile as they began to quote the familiar verse together. "*Be strong and of a good courage; be not afraid, neither be thou dismayed: for* the LORD *thy God is with thee whithersoever thou goest—* Joshua chapter one, verse nine."

"That has been my favorite verse," Victoria Grace said, growing stronger in her spirit. "I've been reciting it daily since Father left."

"I meant what I said before," Todd spoke, as he studied Victoria Grace's face. "I believe that God has given you the strength and courage you need to do what He has called you to do."

Doc Finney joined them and looked at her intently as he spoke. "You know, people always say it takes great courage to fight a war—and it does. But I think it takes almost as much courage to stay home and go on with the everyday things like you and your mother are doing."

"Really?"

"Yes, you are truly one of the most courageous people I've ever met."

Right now she didn't feel courageous, to be sure. "Sometimes I just feel like crawling into the bed and pulling the covers over my head. It's so hard to keep going day after day."

He reached to give her hand a squeeze. "I know that feeling, but we can't give up. We must be strong."

She sighed. "I know you're right." Victoria Grace looked up as one of the wounded began to call out for a drink of water. "I... I must help him." She tried to stand, but still felt a little woozy.

"I'll take care of him." The doctor assured her. "You just rest awhile."

She leaned back against the wall once more and tried to rest, though it was difficult to watch others work when she could not. As she sat there, she thought about what Todd and Doc Finney had told her. She knew in her heart that God had begun to answer her prayers. He was making her strong, courageous, and able to do what she loved—helping others. When she rose, she felt refreshed and eager to help.

Later that evening, after Victoria Grace was finished helping with the wounded, Todd drove her home in the wagon. As she huddled underneath layers of blankets, she looked out across the countryside—nearly dark and still spotted with ice and snow. She prayed for her father, as always, but tonight she prayed for the Gainsborough family as well.

"How long will this war last, Lord?" she asked. She looked up at the skies and sighed.

When she arrived home, Mother greeted her at the door. Victoria Grace ran into her mother's arms, with tears streaming down her face.

"Are you all right, child?" Mother swept her into her arms for a warm embrace.

"Yes, Mother. I'm just sad for the Gainsborough family." They made their way into the parlor, where they sat in front of the fireplace and talked about all that had happened that day.

Mother brushed away tears as she heard the story about Johnny. "I can't imagine losing my son," she whispered. "How awful Mrs. Gainsborough must feel. I will pay her a visit in a few days, to be sure."

"I will come with you," Victoria Grace agreed.

"I am sure they would appreciate that," Mother said. "We'll go after you have had a few days of rest. You look quite exhausted."

Victoria Grace nodded as she let out a quiet yawn and then leaned her head back against the sofa to think about what Mother had said.

"Doc Finney said something rather amazing today, Mother," Victoria Grace said.

"Oh?"

"He said that you and I are just as brave as the men who are fighting in the war."

"Indeed?"

"Yes." She pondered that a minute. "And I think perhaps he is right. We have been very brave, especially you."

"Oh, posh!" Mother said. "Why, I've done nothing extraordinary."

"You have! You have kept the home running smoothly, and worked at the shop as well. I want you to know that I am very grateful for all you have done."

Mother's face beamed with satisfaction. "Thank you, darling. That means a lot to me, and I want you to know how grateful I am for your help. I could never have made it through these months without your assistance. I know Doc Finney feels the same, for he has told me time and again."

"He has?"

"Oh, certainly," Mother said. "Why, every time we see one another, he tells me again what a brilliant assistant you have become." She smiled with a twinkle in her eye. "I knew you could do it."

"Thank you, Mother." Victoria Grace smiled. "I do believe I've surprised even myself. And though I can never be a real doctor, I can go on working alongside Doc Finney for many years to come if he will have me."

"Daughter, I dare say he couldn't do without you!" Mother chuckled and Victoria Grace found herself laughing as well.

A short time later Martha brought in a plate of food—several of Victoria Grace's favorites—and she ate like she had never eaten before.

Finally, when her tummy was full, she lay back on the sofa and watched the bright red and orange flames as they danced merrily in the stone fireplace. They crackled and popped, creating funny little sounds that made her sleepy. Before she knew it, her eyes grew quite heavy and she drifted off to sleep.

As they approached the main street,
Victoria Grace caught sight of something
alarming—a young wounded soldier,
dragging himself into town.

A WOUNDED SOLDIER

$\mathcal{A}$ FEW WEEKS AFTER THE MOORE'S Creek battle, spring arrived in Surry County full force and the wild flowers were spreading across the countryside. The McElyea family was heading into town for their normal Saturday routine with Victoria Grace helping Doc Finney. Mother and Todd would be working at the hattery.

"All of the wounded prisoners are now gone from Doc Finney's," Victoria Grace informed her mother. "Today should be pretty quiet, helping Doc get everything back in order and going over what supplies he needs. Of course, one of the townsfolk might need his attention."

"I think a quiet day would do you good for a change, Daughter," Mother said. "You and the good doctor have certainly had your share of busy days."

"I know," Victoria Grace agreed, "but I really have learned a lot, and look forward to every day I spend with Doc Finney."

"I have a busy day planned," Mother said. "There are many things to be tended to at the hattery. We have more dress orders to fill, and we are working on some new hat fashions."

Victoria Grace bundled up in her coat and scarf before climbing into the wagon. Todd managed the horses, and mother sat to her right with Thomas on her lap. All the way to town, they talked.

"I am so grateful for our wonderful church," Mother said. "The services have been so inspiring, and they bring me such hope."

"Oh, yes!" Todd's eyes lit up as he spoke. "Though I'm exhausted with my workload, I have enjoyed the services because my strength is renewed. And I can truly say that I've grown closer to the Lord than ever before since the war began."

"Amen," Mother added with a smile.

"I like the singing best," Victoria Grace admitted. Truly, the singing was her favorite part of all, though she also loved it when Reverend Compton prayed in his big, booming voice. She also loved thinking about Jesus Christ—the one who had set her free. Every single day when she prayed, she thanked Him for her freedom, and every single day she thanked God for His strength and asked Him for more courage to continue on.

In short order, the McElyea family arrived in town. It was going to be a beautiful sunny day, and the town was already filling with people. Businesses were open, as always, and people moved from shop to shop, making their purchases and chatting with one another.

As they approached the main street, Victoria Grace caught sight of something alarming—a young wounded soldier, dragging himself into town.

She turned to look at Todd with concern in her eyes. "Has there been another battle?"

"Not that I know of," he responded.

"Stop the wagon, Todd, please," she implored.

Her brother had no sooner brought the wagon to a halt than she leapt to the ground.

"Daughter, what are you doing?" her mother cried out.

"I must help him," she said. "Please come for me at Doc Finney's later, if you don't mind."

Mother gave a little nod. "Of course we don't mind. I know you must do what you feel the Lord is calling you to do, and I'm very proud of that. Take care, darling,"

As Victoria Grace drew closer, she saw the extent of the Patriot soldier's wounds. He was bedraggled and dirty. The leg of his pants was torn as well as his jacket, and his side was a bloody mess. The hollows of his eyes were darkened—probably from the blood loss, she guessed—and he was thin as a rail. He glanced her way with a pained expression on his face as their eyes met.

She rushed to his side and tried to help him walk. Within minutes, they were moving at a steady pace in the direction of the doctor's office. Victoria Grace tried to look over his injuries as Doc Finney had taught her to do. The young man, who looked to be about seventeen, was too weak to pay much attention to her. His leg appeared to be mangled, and she could see blood all along the side of his clothes. She began to pray for him at once.

Soon they arrived at Doc Finney's place, and Victoria Grace began to call out for the doctor as soon as she helped the soldier through the door.

"Doc Finney! Doc Finney!"

The doctor's voice rang out from the back office. "What is it, child?"

"I've brought you a wounded soldier," she said as the doctor entered the room.

Doc Finney looked at the young man and understanding registered in his eyes. "Oh my. This one really looks as if he can use our help."

"I'm so v....very th...thirsty," the wounded soldier said.

At once, Victoria Grace went to fetch him a cup of water, which he guzzled down as if he might never drink again.

She spent the next hour or so helping the doctor clean and stitch the soldier's wounds. He had a terrible gash in his side, quite deep, probably from a bayonet wound. "Just like Johnny," she whispered, and his leg was badly wounded as well. Probably from a gunpowder explosion, she guessed.

This time she didn't feel faint, not even once. In fact, the more she worked, the stronger she felt. Doc Finney complimented her on her good work, and she beamed inside and out.

Doc Finney's eyes grew quite serious as he looked the fellow over more closely after stitching the gash in his side.

"Where have you come from, young fellow?"

"S..south Carolina." The soldier mumbled the words, and then his eyes fluttered closed.

"I don't recall hearing of a battle there," Doc Finney said. "How were you wounded?"

The young man's eyes grew large as the pain worsened. "A skirmish. I was jumped."

"Are you a messenger for the Continental Army?"

"Yes sir." He nodded, and then began to groan in pain.

"And you've come all this way on foot?" Doc Finney looked amazed.

"Th…they took my horse," the soldier mumbled.

"You will need much care, young man," the doctor explained, "possibly several weeks."

"Weeks?" The fellow tried to argue, but was too weak.

"Yes." Doc Finney nodded. "You are dehydrated and suffering from malnutrition. These things are as critical as your wounds, which are also quite severe. You can get back to the army after you're healed up and fattened up, but not one day before. The gash in your side will have to be cleaned daily for several weeks so that infection does not set in. Your leg will also need many weeks to heal."

Victoria Grace thought at once of Johnny Gainsborough. If only they could have stopped his infection before it worsened, perhaps he would have lived.

"But sir…" the soldier tried to argue, though his voice was very weak.

"No arguments, son," the good doctor said with a grin. "You will be of no help to your countrymen in this shape. Let's get you healed up first."

"But…" he could barely speak, "I…I've no family here. I don't have a place to stay."

"I will make you a deal," Doc Finney said. "My wife and I have a spare room upstairs that you can use for a few weeks. My wife is the best cook in all of Surry County, at least to my way of thinking. If you'll promise to entertain me with some of your family stories when you're feeling better, you can stay on here with us."

He gave a weak nod, and then drifted off to sleep.

"It will be best to keep this one close by at all times," Doc explained to Victoria Grace. "We will nurse him back to health."

Victoria Grace nodded, suddenly knowing what she must do. She would work day and night if she had to, but she would make absolutely sure that this young soldier pulled through. She would feed him, bring him cups of water, help keep the wound clean and bandaged, and make sure that he received the proper care, no matter how long it took. She didn't want to see another young soldier lose his life. No sir. Not while she was on the job!

David Spence was in God's hands, and God was plenty big enough to take care of him.

A NEW FRIEND

ICTORIA GRACE SPENT THE NEXT several weeks tending to the young soldier. She gave him small bites of food at first, but as the days went on, he was finally able to eat full meals. His wounds were dangerously close to becoming infected at several points, but thanks to her regular care, he seemed to be recovering slowly.

When he was well enough to talk at length, she learned his name: David Spence. As David grew stronger, he told her many stories from his days in the army. She could tell he loved serving in the Continental Army, and could also plainly see that he hoped to return to work as soon as he was strong enough.

"I am anxious to get back to serving in the army," David said. "I'm looking forward to that day."

She gave him another glance. He was just about Trevor's age, and she wondered for a moment if, perhaps, he had met her brother.

They spent many hours talking as Doc and Victoria Grace tended to his wounds. David Spence was full of marvelous stories. He talked about the Continental Army, which he called "a work in progress."

"What does that mean?" Victoria Grace asked him.

He chuckled. "Well, it means we often don't know exactly what we're doing, but we do our very best and learn as we go."

"Then I suppose I am a work in progress as well," she said with a smile, "for I often do not know what I am doing either, but I'm learning."

She flashed a smile at the doctor, who nodded in response. "Indeed," Doc Finney said, "she is a work in progress, but I'm inclined to think we all are."

David's expression grew more serious. "I hear tell the British Army has hired thirty thousand Germans to join their ranks."

"Thirty thousand?" Victoria Grace nearly choked as she said the words. "Why, how many men are in our army? Do we have that many?"

"We are growing in number daily," David said proudly. "I hear tell we've ninety thousand militiamen, though those numbers may vary."

"General Washington leads them all?" Victoria Grace asked.

"He is the commander in chief." David squared his shoulders and smiled. "My brothers and I have met him."

Victoria Grace clamped a hand over her mouth. "Surely you jest."

"No, I'm quite serious. It was a most wonderful experience."

"That's amazing," Victoria Grace said. "I cannot imagine meeting George Washington, our commander in chief. How wonderful that would be."

"He is a godly man who prays for our country—this I know to be true," Doc Finney added. "I have heard as much."

They continued talking about the war, the country's leaders, and the cause of freedom. David Spence proved to be a very knowledgeable boy and a very agreeable one as well. He wore a smile so bright that it seemed to light the room, and though he surely felt some pain as he was healing from his wounds, he never let on.

When David was well enough to get around, Doc Finney changed his dressings and told him to take care while walking about.

David laughed and quickly admitted that he was in no shape to be heading out to the battlefield just yet. "But I would like to spend a little time looking around the town," he said with a friendly smile. "If you think I'm able."

"Just move slowly and carefully," Doc Finney reminded him, "and make sure those stitches remain in place."

Moments later, Victoria Grace and David were outside, making their way across the street. She pointed to the hattery with a proud smile. "That's our store," she explained.

"McElyea's Hattery?" He offered up a polite nod.

"Yes."

"Well, a fellow never knows when he might need a new hat," David teased, "so I guess I should come along and meet your family."

He followed her inside the store, gazing at everything inside.

Mother had a curious look on her face as she looked at him. "You must be David," she said. "I have heard so much about you, and I am glad that you are up and around."

"Thanks to your daughter, I am," David said with a smile. "I am so pleased to make your acquaintance, Mrs. McElyea," David said as he bowed at the waist.

"And yours as well," Mother smiled in amusement, liking him instantly.

After a bit of conversation, she turned her attention to a customer who appeared to be interested in a particular style of hat.

"This three-cornered velvet hat is called a Tricorne," Mother explained to the gentleman. "Very much in fashion."

The fellow with the blonde hair and long, thin nose tried on the hat and then turned about for everyone to see.

"I don't know," he said with a shrug. "What do you think?" He faced Victoria Grace and David.

"Sir," David said with a smile, "you are quite the gentleman in that hat."

"Indeed?"

"Indeed." David's face lit with a smile. "Why, just a few months back, I delivered a message to Philadelphia and noted several of our country's leaders in hats just like that. And of course many of our military men wear the tricorne."

"Truly?" The man suddenly looked very interested.

"Yes," David said, "I've seen tricornes done up with gold or silver lace on them, and some even have feathers."

"Feathers?" The man looked at the hat on his head with great interest. "I might like to have one with feathers."

"Why, sir," Mother said, "I believe I have just the hat for you." She went into the back of the store and returned with a black tricorne, adorned with gold lace and feathers.

The fellow whistled as he took the hat in his hand and immediately tried it on. "Thank you, ma'am, and you can thank this fine fellow right here for helping you make the sale."

As the customer paid for his hat, Victoria Grace showed her new friend around the store.

"You have some very interesting hats here," he said.

"My father is quite good at crafting them," she explained, "especially women's hats. You should see some of the ones he's made. Of course, in his absence, we have other people crafting them. We also have a lot of other things in the store too. Caps and cloaks, bags and pouches, aprons and neckerchiefs, jewelry and shoes… even fine dresses for ladies." She gestured to her mother and the dressmakers in the back room.

"Your mother must be very busy," David said.

"Oh, she is!" she explained. "She tends to the shop, keeps the books, and cares for all of us and the house…" Victoria Grace gave her mother an admiring smile, and then turned her attentions back to David, adding one final thought on the matter. "Thankfully, we have several other women who work for us as well."

"That's nice." He looked at the seamstresses as they worked, then gave Victoria Grace a smile. "Do you sew?" he asked Victoria Grace.

"Hardly!" she said with a laugh. "My stitches are deplorable." She lifted her hands and showed them to him. "Mother teases that I'm all thumbs."

"Ah, I see." He chuckled. "So sewing is not what you were created to do."

"Indeed not." Victoria Grace put on a more serious face. "My calling is elsewhere. As you know, I work with Doc Finney most of the time when I am not in school."

"You do have a gift of caring for others. That I have noticed. Do you intend to keep working with the doctor?" David asked with a smile.

Just as she opened her mouth to answer him, Todd joined them.

"My sister could make a fine doctor one day," Todd bragged. "Why, she can be anything she wants to be if she puts her mind to it!"

Victoria Grace beamed with pride.

"With the Lord's help, we can be all He has created us to be," David added. "That's why I plan to return to the battlefield as soon as possible. Surely, God is on my side and will go with me."

Victoria Grace thought about her new friend's words. Though it made her sad to think about David returning to war, she knew he was a fine soldier. Somehow she also knew—though she wasn't sure how—that she would one day see him again. Somehow, just knowing that gave her a sense of peace. David Spence was in God's hands, and God was plenty big enough to take care of him.

Victoria Grace met him outside with a shout, "Father!" She threw her arms around him and embraced him with tears streaming down her face.

THE HOMECOMING

AUGUST 1776

*M*ONTHS PASSED AND THE WAR RAGED on. True to his word, David Spence returned to the Continental Army, healthy and strong once more. Victoria Grace missed him terribly, and prayed for him just as she did for all the brave men.

Day after day, Victoria Grace waited for news from the frontlines about Father and Trevor. Letters hardly ever came anymore, but she tried to keep her faith instead of giving up hope.

As August approached, the summer sun blazed hot in the sky above. Victoria Grace continued to make the journey into town several days a week to help Doc Finney. In her spare time, she and Adeline spent the hot days cooling off in the Yadkin River, but with school starting soon, she knew things were bound to change.

Todd and Mother kept the hattery running strong. Father would be so proud when he returned home.

About a week into August, the family received a letter from David Spence. With the letter in her hand, Victoria Grace made her way out across their property to a large tree. She sat beneath it, opened the letter, and began to read.

David spoke of something fascinating, something almost too good to be true. She read the letter again and again, trying to understand all of his words.

Dear McElyea family,

I am writing this letter from Long Island, New York, where we are preparing for battle. The British have landed in this area, some thirty thousand strong. Please keep us in your prayers as we prepare to meet them head-on.

Our spirits are high, in spite of the upcoming battle. We have received wonderful news, news that encourages us to fight on. We have just learned that the Declaration of Independence, crafted by Mr. Thomas Jefferson, has been signed. The words in this Declaration have energized me, particularly the section that reads, "We hold these truths to be self-evident, that all men are created equal, that they are endowed by their Creator with certain unalienable rights, that among these are Life, Liberty, and the pursuit of Happiness."

Life, liberty, and the pursuit of happiness—these are the things we long for! And these are the things I will continue to fight for. I feel sure there are many battles ahead, but we will face them with renewed courage.

I know that you are just as courageous as we. Daily, I think of your wonderful family and pray for you all. I look forward to the day when we can see each other again. Perhaps that day will come soon.

Your faithful friend in the Lord,
David Spence

"Life, liberty, and the pursuit of happiness." Victoria Grace thought about those words as she spoke them aloud. The men on the battleground fought for life and liberty, so that they could be free.

Men like Father and Trevor. Men like David Spence.

Right away she thought back to the conversation she'd had with her father that day over a year and a half ago. What was it he had said, again?

Some things are worth fighting for.

Now she understood what he'd meant—really, truly understood it.

Victoria Grace stood and brushed the dirt from her skirt, and then made her way back to the house. Once she reached the door, Mother met her with another letter in her hand.

"I've just had word from Father!" she exclaimed.

"Really?"

"Yes, and listen to this. He is coming home soon."

"When, Mother? When?" Victoria Grace bounced up and down in excitement. Right away her smile faded. "Oh, but I hope he hasn't been wounded. He hasn't, has he?"

"Not wounded," Mother explained, "though he has been very ill. Smallpox."

"Smallpox?" Victoria Grace bit her lip, but tried to be brave. "Smallpox can be very dangerous. Are you sure he will be all right?"

Mother gave her a tender smile, and reached to grab her hand for a squeeze. "Why, when he arrives home, he will receive the best care possible. After all, you will be here to help tend to his needs, and you are a skilled medical assistant."

"Yes!" Her excitement grew. "That's true. Doc Finney can give me instructions, and I can care for him."

Right away she felt better about things.

Less than a week later, Father returned home. He was weakened by the illness, and required Todd's help to get out of the wagon. Victoria Grace met him outside with a shout, "Father!" She threw her arms around him and embraced him with tears streaming down her face.

"Daughter, I've missed you so!" His voice was very weak, but he managed to lean down to plant several kisses on the top of her head. "And Mary, my darling bride!" He reached to wrap his wife in his arms. She rested her head against his shoulder.

"I can't believe it," she kept saying. "I simply cannot believe it. You're here, at last! But I'm so sorry you're ill, Lodwick. So sorry, indeed."

"I'll be fine in no time, Mary. And I have Victoria Grace to help me recover, after all. I hear tell there is no finer medical assistant in Surry County."

Father moved to take Victoria Grace's hands, and he looked intently into her eyes. "Todd told me how bravely you were caring for the wounded soldiers, and I want you to know how proud I am of you."

Victoria Grace's face beamed as her father embraced her once again.

"Father, come inside and see Baby Thomas. He is not such a baby anymore," Victoria Grace said as she walked with her father into the house.

Minutes later they sat together in the parlor. Father rested on the sofa, looking pale and much thinner than Victoria Grace remembered. She vowed to do her best to care for him until he was healthy again.

"Martha has baked a cake!" Mother said.

"Martha?" Father looked confused. "Who is Martha?"

"Oh, that's right!" Mother put her hand to her mouth, astonished, "Why I'd forgotten that you don't even know Martha Moore. She's been such a help since you've been gone. I hired her just after you left. I don't know what I would have done without her."

"Mary and Martha—together in the same house." Father gave a weak smile. "Just like in the Bible!"

Just then Martha came into the room with a large pound cake on a lovely silver tray. "Welcome home, Mr. McElyea!" she cheered. "I baked your favorite."

"However did you know?" he asked, looking at the cake in awe.

"Why, your wife told me. 'Pound cake for my Lodwick,' she said. 'For that is his favorite.'" Martha gave him a grin. "And there's nothing like a little of my pound cake to bring strength to your bones."

"What about tea? Good strong tea?" He asked with a twinkle in his eye.

"Oh, yes sir. I'll be right back with the tea. Yes I will."

She scurried off to fetch the large silver teapot and returned moments later. Then, as the whole family ate cake and drank tea, Mother asked about how father was feeling.

"It will take months before I'm truly healthy and well," he explained. "At least, that's what the doctor says.

After I have regained my strength, I hope to return to my regiment."

"Please no, Father!" Victoria Grace cried out. She could hardly imagine her father leaving again. He reached to pat her hand. "You will nurse me back to health," he said, "and then we will see."

"We are thrilled to have you home—even if it is just for a little while," Mother said. "How I wish I could see Trevor as well."

"You would be so proud of your son, Mary," Father said. "He's the bravest soldier fighting in the Continental, I dare say."

"Truly?" Mother asked.

"Oh yes, indeed. He's faced down many of the Redcoats, and he came out a victor every time," Father explained. He went on to explain that Trevor had received a slight wound to his leg last spring, but had recovered quickly.

"Thank goodness for that," Mother said. "Thank goodness."

"He will return home soon, Lord willing," Father assured her, "but after the war, he plans to move on to Pennsylvania. I do believe he has fallen in love with the Philadelphia area, and plans to study law."

"Study law? My Trevor?" Mother looked so proud.

"Yes, that's right," Father said.

Martha drew close and poured them some more tea. "I wonder if you know my husband, Bradford Moore," she asked.

"Bradford Moore? A tall fellow with large brown eyes and a smile as wide as the Delaware River?"

Martha beamed from ear to ear. "Yes sir. He's my husband, and I miss him something terrible. I haven't heard from him in a while."

"Ah, I see." Victoria Grace couldn't help but notice that Father's gaze shifted down to the ground. "I do know your husband. Quite well, in fact. He was in my regiment. He is quite a brave soldier, to be sure."

"What do you know of him?" Martha asked, drawing closer. "If you don't mind my asking."

Father seemed to stammer a bit as he answered, "I, um… well, I do know that he was wounded several weeks back."

"No!" Martha nearly dropped the teapot as the fear registered on her face. "Is he…." Tears filled her eyes and she could not finish the sentence.

"He is alive," Father said, "and the wound was not the result of battle, but rather an attempt to save another soldier's life."

"My Bradford… is a hero?"

"Indeed. Though I am sorry to tell you that he has suffered a terrible wound to his shoulder and has lost the use of his right arm, at least for now."

"No!" Martha looked as if she might faint, and Mother rushed to her rescue.

"Be assured, he is a strong man," Father said. "Many were the times I listened to Bradford talk about his beautiful wife. Of course, I had no idea I would one day meet her."

Martha's face lit into a smile. "He spoke of me?"

"Every day! He told me that you are much like the Martha mentioned in the Bible—always working hard for others."

Martha giggled. "I do love that man."

"We love all of our brave fighting men," Mother was quick to add.

Father went on to tell many stories of his days in the Continental Army. Victoria Grace listened intently to every word. She was so happy to have Father at home.

As their conversation finally drew to a close, she leaned back in her chair and closed her eyes, thinking about all of Father's stories. She pictured the battlegrounds in her mind. Heard the sounds of the musket fire and saw the bayonets as they cut through the air. Imagined the soldiers—men like her father and brother—running toward the frontlines, prepared to fight...to fight for *her* freedom. What a price they had all paid! And how brave they had been! And how courageous she now felt as well!

Just then her father reached over and took her hand. "Daughter, I have something to say to you."

Her eyes flew open and she gazed up at him with a smile. "Yes, Father?"

He began to quote the verse he'd taught her since childhood: *"Be strong and of a good courage; be not afraid, neither be thou dismayed: for the* LORD *thy God is with thee whithersoever thou goest."*

Victoria Grace's heart began to beat in excitement as she thought about those words. They meant so much to her now.

Father gave her hand a squeeze and whispered, "Do you understand it now, child? Do you understand such courage?"

"Oh, Father, I do!" She jumped up from the chair and leapt into his outstretched arms. "I truly, truly do!"

"That's why I chose that particular story—so that you can learn from others in our family how to put your trust in God and be courageous."

COURAGE

*S*ARA ELIZABETH LOOKED AT GRAND DOLL in amazement as she finished the story. "Grand Doll, I didn't know about Victoria Grace. Was she really someone from our family?"

"Indeed," her grandmother said with a smile, "and she was truly one of the most courageous girls who ever lived, don't you think?"

All of the children agreed.

"But you didn't finish the story," one of the boys said. "Who won the war?"

"Ah." Grand Doll looked at the children with excitement in her eyes. "Well, the battles raged back and forth, back and forth. The British would win one, then the Patriots. On and on it went. But in the end…"

The children all sat at attention in their desks, ready to hear.

"In the end," Grand Doll said, "the American colonists won their independence."

"Is that what we celebrate on the fourth of July?" Sara Elizabeth asked. "Our independence from the British?"

"That's right," Grand Doll said, "and if those brave Patriots hadn't taken a stand for what they believed, then we wouldn't have the freedom we now enjoy."

The school bell rang, and Mrs. Frazier dismissed the students for the day. As they left, each one stopped to thank Grand Doll for her story.

"That was a lot of fun, Mrs. Clark," one of the girls said. "You sure make history come alive!"

"Thank you for the cool story," Chandler agreed.

"Yes," Mrs. Frazier added. "You've made this a wonderful day for the children, Mrs. Clark. I do believe you would have made an excellent teacher. Thank you so much for coming and sharing your family's story."

After the room cleared out, Sara Elizabeth looked into Grand Doll's eyes. "I can be brave just like Victoria Grace, isn't that right?"

"Yes." Grand Doll nodded and a little smile lit her face. "That's why I chose that particular story—so that you can learn from others in our family how to put your trust in God and be courageous."

"I do miss Mama," Sara Elizabeth said, "but this new school can be fun too. I think I can be brave."

"Starting tomorrow?"

Sara Elizabeth nodded. "May I ask you one more question? I want to know something else about Victoria Grace."

"Of course." Grand Doll took her by the hand, and they walked together from the classroom as they talked.

"What ever happened to Victoria Grace? When she grew up, I mean. Did she ever get married and have children?"

Grand Doll smiled. "Oh my, yes, and you might be surprised to hear who she married."

"Who?"

"David Spence."

"No way! The Continental soldier?"

"Yes," Grand Doll said. "David returned to the battle-field where he fought valiantly until the war ended. Then David returned to Surry County, where he married Victoria Grace, and they started a family of their own." Grand Doll's eyes sparkled as she continued on. "And Victoria Grace worked alongside Doc Finney until the day he died. Then when the next doctor arrived in town, she worked with him as well."

"Wow."

"There's a lot to be learned from the stories of those who walked before us, Sara Elizabeth. And remember what Victoria Grace's father told her...there are some things in life you have to fight for."

"Like what, Grand Doll?"

"Like your freedom. Freedom still comes at a cost. Early Americans had their struggles, but we have ours today too. There are some people who don't believe that Americans should be free to worship or even talk about God in public places, places like this school."

"Really?"

"Yes. The Ten Commandments, which were on the wall in my schoolhouse as a child, have been removed."

Sara Elizabeth looked around. "You're right. I don't see them anywhere."

"When I was a girl," Grand Doll continued, "we used to start each school day with prayer as well as the pledge to the flag."

"You did?"

"Yes." Grand Doll nodded. "These days it's a little more difficult for children to take a stand and tell others what they believe, but it's still possible. I hope you have enough courage to share your faith with others, even when it seems really hard."

"I will, Grand Doll. I promise. If Victoria Grace could be brave, I can too."

"That's my girl." Her grandmother reached down and planted a kiss on her forehead. "I'm so proud of you."

"Thank you, Grand Doll. I'm proud of you too."

"I have one more thing to share with you," Grand Doll said as she reached into her bag once again. She held up the big black Bible she had read from earlier and laid it in Sara Elizabeth's arms.

"This old Bible came from the memory trunk, and do you know who it belonged to?" Grand Doll asked with a twinkle in her eye.

Sara Elizabeth shook her head no and awaited her answer.

"It was Victoria Grace's family Bible, and her marriage to David Spence is recorded in it. As the Bible was passed down from generation to generation, many of her relatives were also listed in it."

"Wow!" Sara Elizabeth exclaimed, her eyes wide in awe. She looked at the Bible and carefully turned the pages, reading the names of relatives from long ago. She could hardly believe that Victoria Grace had read from this very Bible. She reverently gave the Bible back to Grand Doll and gave her a big hug.

"Thank you for coming to see me today, Grand Doll," Sara Elizabeth said as she reached for her grandmother's hand and started walking down the hall.

As they walked along, Grand Doll began to sing, her beautiful voice ringing out against the now-empty hallways.

His peace is sufficient for me, praise God.
His peace is sufficient for me.
When my God is near, I cannot fear.
His peace is sufficient for me.

"What's that you're singing?" Sara Elizabeth asked. "I've never heard it before."

"It's a little song I wrote. Do you like it?"

"I do. Will you sing it again?"

As her grandmother began to sing the beautiful song once more, Sara Elizabeth listened closely to the words, especially this part: "When my God is near, I cannot fear."

The Bible verse Grand Doll had shared earlier from Joshua 1:9 came to her mind at once: *Be strong and of a good courage; be not afraid, neither be thou dismayed: for the LORD thy God is with thee whithersoever thou goest.*

"I can be strong and courageous," Sara Elizabeth whispered, giving Grand Doll's hand a squeeze. "Not just at school, but every day of my life."

With a skip in her step, she headed out the door.

Fun Facts
and More

Fun Facts From History

§ If the Revolutionary War had not been fought, America might still be under British rule today.

§ A "patriot" is someone who loves and/or defends his or her country. Revolutionary Patriots loved their country and wanted to be free from British rule so that they could govern themselves. Patriots were also known as "Whigs."

§ The "Tories" (also called "Loyalists") were those people who supported the British during the Revolutionary War period.

§ British soldiers who fought in the Revolutionary War period were called "Redcoats" or "Lobsterbacks."

§ People who changed their mind about which side they were on were called "Turncoats."

§ The most famous "Turncoat" during the Revolutionary War was Benedict Arnold, who started out supporting the colonists and ended up siding with the British. To this day, people think of the word "traitor" when they hear his name.

§ The thirteen original colonies were Massachusetts, Virginia, New Hampshire, Maryland, Connecticut, Rhode Island, Delaware, North Carolina, South Carolina, New Jersey, New York, Pennsylvania, and Georgia.

§ During the Revolutionary War, women took over their husbands' positions back at home (running homes and businesses).

§ George Washington, who served as the commander in chief of the American forces during the war, became our country's first president in 1789.

§ The Revolutionary War began on April 19, 1775 at Lexington and Concord and ended with the signing of the Treaty of Paris in 1783.

§ America celebrates it independence on the 4th of July—the day the Declaration of Independence was signed.

§ Is freedom really free?

§ What does it mean to be courageous?

§ What is the most courageous thing you have ever done?

§ What would have happened if the colonists had not taken a stand against the British?

§ Have you ever had to take a stand? Explain.

§ What does it mean to have "life, liberty, and the pursuit of happiness"?

§ What happened during the Boston Tea Party?

§ Who sewed our first American flag?

§ Why was it important for our country's founders to write a "declaration" of independence?

§ The Declaration of Independence states that all men (and women) are created equal. How do you feel about that? What does the Bible say about that?

§ Do you know any old hymns? Ask your parents or grandparents if they know any and if they will sing some to you.

EBSTER'S DICTIONARY DEFINES *courage* as: "mental or moral strength to venture, persevere, and withstand danger, fear, or difficulty. Courage implies firmness of mind and will in the face of danger or extreme difficulty."[1]

In Joshua 1:7, God speaks these words to His servant, Joshua: *"Only be strong and very courageous, that you may observe to do according to all the law which Moses My servant commanded you; do not turn from it to the right hand or to the left, that you may prosper wherever you go"* (NKJV).

A good example of *courage* comes from the life of Esther (Hadassah). In the book of Esther, chapter 4:13-16, we read, *And Mordecai told them to answer Esther: "Do not think in your heart that you will escape in the king's palace any more than all the other Jews. For if you remain completely silent at this time, relief and deliverance*

---

[1]*Merriam Webster's Collegiate Dictionary*, 11th Edition, s.v. "Courage."

will arise for the Jews from another place, but you and your father's house will perish. Yet who knows whether you have come to the kingdom for such a time as this." Then Esther told them to reply to Mordecai: "Go, gather all the Jews who are present in Shushan, and fast for me; neither eat nor drink for three days, night or day. My maids and I will fast likewise. And so I will go to the king, which is against the law; and if I perish, I perish!" (NKJV) She gathered *courage* from God and went before the king to save her people, knowing that entering into his presence without being called for could result in death. That's real *courage*.

Another example would be having the *courage* to forgive someone who has hurt you. *"But if you do not forgive, neither will your Father in heaven forgive your trespasses"* (Mark 11:26 NKJV). Think about a time when you had to forgive someone (maybe even today), and God gave you the *courage* to forgive him or her and not think about it anymore. How were you able to handle it?

There may be times in our own lives when we will be called upon to stand up for the Gospel of Christ. At the risk of embarrassment or even hurt, will we stand in *courage* or turn away?

Consider the story of Stephen in Acts 7:55-60. *But he* [Stephen], *being full of the Holy Spirit, gazed into heaven and saw the glory of God, and Jesus standing at the right of God, and said, "Look! I see the heavens opened and the*

Son of Man standing at the right hand of God!" Then they [the elders and scribes among the Jews] *cried out with a loud voice, stopped their ears, and ran at him with one accord; and they cast him out of the city and stoned him. And the witnesses laid down their clothes at the feet of a young man named Saul* [Paul]. *And they stoned Stephen as he was calling on God and saying, "Lord Jesus, receive my spirit." Then he knelt down and cried out with a loud voice, "Lord, do not charge them with this sin"* (NKJV).

Has there been a time in your own life when you had to stand strong for Jesus when others seemed to be against you? For us, *courage* has many faces. We may not be called upon to give up our lives for the Gospel, but we may be called on in other ways:

1. It can be as simple as studying hard for a test, praying for guidance, and leaving the results to God. Can you think of a time when God showed you how faithful He is when you had the *courage* to leave the results to Him?

    Don't be impatient. Wait for the Lord, and he will come and save you! Be brave, stout-hearted, and courageous. Yes, wait and he will help you (Psalm 27:14 TLB).

2. It could be saying no to a temptation from someone who asks you to lie to your parents or your teacher to cover up for them. How

did you deal with this type of situation? Did you experience *courage* rising up in you to do the right thing?

But remember this—the wrong desires that come into your life aren't anything new and different. Many others have faced exactly the same problems before you.

And no temptation is irresistible. You can trust God to keep the temptation from becoming so strong that you can't stand up against it, for he has promised this and will do what he says. He will show you how to escape temptation's power so that you can bear up patiently against it (1 Corinthians 10:13 TLB).

3. Or it could be saying, "I was wrong and you were right." That takes a lot of *courage*. Sometimes our pride gets in the way. If we always want to be right, we may miss out on learning from others who may have more knowledge or wisdom than we do at the time. How are you able to handle correction from someone else? It takes real *courage* to admit our mistakes.

Pride leads to arguments; be humble, take advice and become wise (Proverbs 13:10 TLB).

Victoria Grace needed courage for many things in this story. Can you name what they were and how she received the courage to overcome them?

_____

_____

_____

_____

Can you find some other scriptures in the Bible that speak about courage?

_____

_____

_____

_____

Has there been a time in your own life when you have needed courage to overcome an obstacle?

_____

_____

_____

_____

Pick someone from American history who showed great courage and write about him or her.

Mark Twain said, "Courage is not the lack of fear. It is acting in spite of it." Some people believe that if they have fear, then they don't have courage. That is not actually true. True courage is facing your fears and acting in spite of them.

"Only be strong and very courageous...then you will make your way prosperous, and then you will have good success" (Joshua 1:7-8 NKJV).

The presence of God is what gives you courage.

The One-Room Schoolhouse

NE-ROOM SCHOOLHOUSES WERE A VERY important part of early America from the 1700s all the way into the 1900s. In fact, there are still a few one-room schoolhouses around today. How were one-room schoolhouses different from your schools today? Let's go back in time and take a peek at what it was like to go to school in the one-room schoolhouse.

The schoolhouse was usually built in the center of a county or town and often also served as the church. Children of all ages came from miles around on foot, horseback, or wagon to have school together in one room.

There was a potbelly wood stove at the center or back of the room, and children carried wood to school in winter months to keep the stove burning so the classroom would be warm. The teacher's desk was at the front of the classroom. When blackboards were available, there was one very large one at the front or side of the classroom. It was the children's job to wash the blackboard every night and to clap the dust out of the erasers. Water had to be brought into the classroom where crocks were filled for drinking and basins for washing hands. Most schools only had benches for the children to sit on, but some schools were lucky enough to have desks the children could use when writing their lessons.

School supplies were much different for the children in the one-room schoolhouse. Writing paper and ink were scarce, so most of the work was done by recitation. If paper was available, children used quills and inkwells. When slates became available, children brought their own slate and chalk. In the earliest school days, books were not as easy to get as they are today. Many times children brought books from home—often the books their parents had used as children. These books were used not only for learning to read, but also as lessons for a variety of other subjects. In addition, there was usually a Bible in the classroom, probably the *King James Version*.

As the children arrived at school and visited with their friends, the teacher or teacher's helper rang the bell for the school day to begin. Children brought their lunches in pails or buckets. Mornings started with a prayer, the pledge of allegiance (after America became a nation), and maybe some singing. Then the children learned the three "R's"—reading, writing, and arithmetic.

Lessons usually started with reading aloud. The teacher divided the students into groups according to their reading ability. Then she called each group to her desk to read aloud. In the 1700s, children read from the *Hornbook* and *New England Primer*. In the late 1700s, Noah Webster wrote the *Blue-backed Speller,* which was used for over 100 years. The *McGuffey Reader* was used in the 1800s. Children also recited scriptures from the Bible. The teacher moved through all of the groups until everyone had completed their reading.

After reading, there was usually a break for recess. After the break, the students would begin their math or "ciphering," as it was called back then. The children were expected to master simple addition and subtraction before moving on to more difficult skills such as multiplication, division, and maybe even geometry and algebra. After the math lessons, it was time for lunch. The children could eat inside or go outside for lunch. After lunch, they played games. Some of the games they played are still popular today—jump rope, tag, and kite flying. Other games like spinning tops, marbles, and lawn bowling are thought of as old-fashioned.

After lunch and recess, the children met inside to study other subjects the teacher chose—science, history, geography, and writing. Spelling bees were also very popular. It was also common for the older students to help the younger students with their lessons. In some schools, the younger children were released from school

early so the teacher could concentrate on teaching the older children higher education skills.

The school day was often long and rigorous, and in addition to learning to the best of their ability, every child was expected to do their fair share in keeping the classroom neat. After the school day, the students helped clean the classroom and get it ready for the following day. The children then went home where they probably had daily "chores" to do.

Life back then was very different from what we experience today, but it is always nice to go back and "visit" the past so we can learn from it. It also helps us to appreciate what we have today.

O YOU LIKE TO PLAY SCHOOL? HAVE you ever wondered what it was like to go to school in a one-room schoolhouse? With a little help, you can recreate it and experience the fun of playing school the old-fashioned way…in a one-room schoolhouse. If you are a *Little House on the Prairie* fan, you have seen the one-room schoolhouse—now you can enjoy the fun of recreating it for yourself.

To start the fun, dress up as the children did back then. It is fun to dress the part to help you experience what it was like. Do you have a colonial or pioneer costume? If not, find a long prairie skirt and white blouse (for girls) or trousers, shirt, and suspenders (for boys) to help put you in the mood.

Next you will need to gather some of the items the children used at the one-room schoolhouse. Let's start with what the students took from home. All the children carried their lunches in a lunch bucket or pail. Refer to the following pages for instructions on making your own "lunch pail." Be sure to fill your pail with foods they would have eaten back then. Many children took leftover meats, cheese, bread, and fruit. They covered their lunch buckets or pails with cloths to keep the food fresh. They also took a jar of water or lemonade to drink.

Next let's work on the school supplies. The children took their own slates, chalk, paper, quill, and ink, if available, and any books they might have. Find the *King James Version* of the Bible and add it to your school supplies. Ask your mom if she has any old school books such as the *McGuffey Reader* or *New England Primer*. If you don't have any of those, don't worry—the following pages will show you how to make your own *Hornbook* and *New England Primer*. Half the fun of playing school is getting all of your supplies together.

Now you should have most of your supplies ready for school—a lunch pail full of healthy foods, covered with a napkin or bandanna. A small slate and chalk, maybe a pen and inkwell, and books, including the Bible, the *Hornbook*, the *New England Primer*, and maybe even another reader if your mom has one.

You will also need to have games ready for recess. Children back then played many of the same games that you play today, but they also played some games you might consider old-fashioned. They played jump rope, tag, and had many different kinds of races, such as potato-sack and three-legged races. Some of the more old-fashioned games they played were marbles, spinning tops, lawn bowling, and blind man's bluff. I am sure you can find a jump rope, a handkerchief to play blind man's bluff, and maybe even some marbles. Add this to your "one-room schoolhouse" supplies to make your day more authentic and fun.

Someone will need to play the teacher. This is a fun role to play, so take turns and let everyone have a chance.

Here is a schedule that students could have followed in the one-room schoolhouse:

§ Mornings began with prayers, pledges, and maybe even a song. After that, the first lesson was usually reading. The children read aloud from the Bible, the *Primers,* and *Hornbooks.* Once all of the students had read aloud, they took a short recess.

§ After recess, the students usually worked on their math. This was usually done on their slates. Simple skills such as addition and subtraction were accomplished first before moving on to more difficult skills. Once math was completed, the children took a break for lunch.

§ Lunch, of course, was one of their favorite times of day—much like it is for you. The children had worked up quite an appetite by that time, and they really enjoyed their lunch. Next they played many of the games mentioned above. The girls played jump rope,

and usually the boys played marbles.

Sometimes they all joined together for a game of tag or blind man's bluff. Many times the teacher joined in and played as well.

§ After lunch, the children moved on to other subjects such as science, history, and writing. They practiced writing on paper with pen (quills) and ink. They also looked forward to spelling bees and worked hard to do well. You may want to include a spelling bee when you are recreating the old-fashioned school day.

§ After lessons were completed for the day, the children cleaned up the classroom and went home. Make sure your slate is wiped clean, your books are neatly stacked, and your lunch pail is clean.

Playing "One-Room Schoolhouse" is fun, and also allows you to experience what school was like for children back in early America. Although the classroom, clothing, and school supplies were much different than they are today, one thing remains the same. Children go to school to learn and have fun.

Enjoy playing "One-Room Schoolhouse"!

MAKE YOUR OWN LUNCH PAIL

To make a lunch pail similar to the ones the children carried to the one-room schoolhouse, ask your parents for an empty 3-pound coffee can. Peel off the label, exposing the plain, silver metal. With your parents' help, punch a hole on both sides of the can near the top rim. Cut a wire to make a handle for the "pail." Insert the wire in the holes on both sides of the can, and twist the ends securely to form the handle.

Children placed their lunches inside the metal pail and covered it with a cloth. For a cloth, you can use a bandanna, handkerchief, or napkin. Children's lunches consisted mostly of fruit, leftover meats, cheese, and bread. (No processed or snack food allowed.) Water or lemonade can be carried in a glass jar with a metal lid.

MAKE YOUR OWN HORNBOOK

What is a hornbook? Hornbooks were used in the 1700s and even the 1600s because paper was hard to come by and expensive as well. They were not really books at all, but a piece of wood with paper attached to it. The wood was usually in the shape of a paddle, similar to a large spatula or hand mirror. A sheet of sturdy paper attached to the paddle contained the alphabet, blends of letters, and a prayer. It was then covered with a thin layer of cow's horn to protect the paper—hence, the name "horn" book. Hornbooks were made so children could use them over and over again, memorizing, reading, and tracing the letters and words with a sharp stick or dry quill pen. The students used hornbooks to learn the alphabet and letter blends and to help them learn to read by studying the words of a familiar prayer.

Use the following steps to make your own hornbook:

Step 1: Find a wooden clipboard, a piece of card-board, or even a piece of wood for the base of your hornbook.

Step 2: Find a sturdy piece of paper. At the top, neatly write the letters of the alphabet—both small and capital letters. In the middle, write some letter blends such as "ch," "sh," "tr," etc. Near the bottom, write the words of the *Lord's Prayer*.

Step 3: Attach the paper to the clipboard and cover with wax paper.

Step 4: Some children decorated their hornbooks. You can decorate yours with extra buttons, pieces of leather, and jewels. Find a sharp stick or quill pen that you can use to trace the letters.

Now you are ready to go over the alphabet, learn your blends, and read the prayer.

The *New England Primer* is a textbook that was used by students in the 1700s and 1800s. Since schools were greatly influenced by religion, the book combined the alphabet with Bible scriptures. Each letter of the alphabet began with a Bible verse or phrase, followed by a picture. It also contained many religious questions and answers, placing particular emphasis on sin and God's judgment. The end of the book contained a prayer. The *New England Primer* was the first book to include the familiar children's bedtime prayer, "Now I Lay Me Down to Sleep."

Use the following steps to make your own *New England Primer*:

Step 1: Start with about 30–50 sheets of loose-leaf paper. To bind together, punch 3 holes spaced evenly apart in the left side of the paper. Punch 3 holes (also in the left side) in 2 pieces of cardboard or sturdy paper the same size as the loose-leaf papers. Place these pieces on the stack of papers—one on top and the other on the bottom. Tie each hole with string or leather, binding the cover, paper, and back into one book. Print and color the name *New England Primer* on the front cover.

Step 2: Begin the first section of the book with the alphabet and verses. Label each page with a letter from the alphabet in large print. Find a verse from the Bible that begins with that letter, or make up your own phrase that begins with that letter. Then illustrate each letter with a picture. You should have 26 pages for the 26 letters of the alphabet. Here is an example for the letters "A" and "B":

A: Made-up phrase: Angels sing to Christ the King. (Illustrate with a picture of an angel.)

B: Bible verse: *"Blessed are the pure in heart, for they will see God"* (Matthew 5:8 NIV). (Illustrate with a picture of a heart.)

Complete the entire alphabet. Be creative and have fun.

Step 3: Next you are ready for the second section of the book. Use the next few pages for questions and answers about God. Here is an example:

Question: Why did God give His only begotten Son that whosoever believes in Him would not perish but have life everlasting?

Answer: God gave his Son because He loved the world (see John 3:16).

Step 4: The last section of the book included a prayer. You can make up your own prayer or use this child's bedtime prayer:

Now I lay me down to sleep,
I pray the Lord my soul to keep.
If I should die before I wake,
I pray the Lord my soul to take.

Step 5: Leave a few blank pages at the end of the book to be used for extra writing when you are playing school.

ELEANOR CLARK CONCEIVED THE IDEA for *The Eleanor Series* while researching her family's rich American history. Motivated by her family lineage, which had been traced back to the early 17th century, a God-ordained idea emerged: the legacy left by her ancestors provided the perfect tool to reach today's children with the timeless truths of patriotism, godly character, and miracles of faith. Through her own family's stories, she instills in children a love of God and country, along with a passion for history. With that in mind, she set out to craft this collection of novels for the youth of today. Each story in *The Eleanor Series* focuses on a particular character trait, and is laced with the pioneering spirit of one of Eleanor's true-to-life family members. These captivating stories span generations, are historically accurate, and highlight the nation's Christian heritage of faith. Twenty-first century readers—both children and parents—are sure to relate to these amazing character-building stories of young American's while learning Christian values and American history.

Look for all of these books in the Eleanor Series:

Christmas Book—*Eleanor Jo: A Christmas to Remember*
ISBN-10: 0-9753036-6-X
ISBN-13: 978-0-9753036-6-5

Available in 2007

Book One—*Mary Elizabeth: Welcome to America*
ISBN-10: 0-9753036-7-8
ISBN-13: 978-0-9753036-7-2

Book Two—*Victoria Grace: Courageous Patriot*
ISBN-10: 0-9753036-8-6
ISBN-13: 978-0-9753036-8-9

Book Three—*Katie Sue: Heading West*
ISBN-10: 0-9788726-0-6
ISBN-13: 978-0-9788726-0-1

Book Four—*Sarah Jane: Liberty's Torch*
ISBN-10: 0-9753036-9-4
ISBN-13: 978-0-9753036-9-6

Book Five—*Eleanor Jo: The Farmer's Daughter*
ISBN-10: 0-9788726-1-4
ISBN-13: 978-0-9788726-1-8

Book Six—*Melanie Ann: A Legacy of Love*
ISBN-10: 0-9788726-2-2
ISBN-13: 978-0-9788726-2-5

Visit our Web site at: www.eleanorseries.com

About the Author

ELEANOR CLARK LIVES IN central Texas with Lee, her husband of over 50 years, and as matriarch of the family, she is devoted to her 5 children, 17 grandchildren, and 4 great grandchildren.

Born the daughter of a Texas sharecropper and raised in the Great Depression, Eleanor was a female pioneer in crossing economic, gender, educational, and corporate barriers. An executive for one of America's most prestigious ministries, Eleanor later founded her own highly successful consulting firm. Her appreciation of her American and Christian heritage comes to life along with her exciting and colorful family history in the youth fiction series, *The Eleanor Series*.